I0640115

TRAVELER FOR

Qty _____ Date _____

Qty _____ Date _____

Cut By: _____

Scanned By

Scanned P

Maxwell Edison whistled his favorite tune, the one from which he derived his name, while he strolled back inside the bank. In no particular rush at all, Maxwell winked at a cute teller hiding behind an overturned desk, as if completely unawares of the situation and with the same casual confidence he would have displayed winking at a girl in a pub.

Maxwell obviously wasn't here for the cash - he planned to burn it all anyway, and loose the ashes on Lake Shore Drive for shiggles. But he needed to pass the time, and he thought it might help him get in character, so he strolled into the vault passed the enormous, sad metal door lying pathetically on the ground, impotent to protect its treasures after Maxwell effortlessly ripped it loose and tossed it aside with the slightest whim.

He grabbed a large brick of cash - it sort of delighted him to see the money was wrapped, packed, and taped into bundles like any other product or merchandise - and walked it over to the armored car. The car was already pretty full from its other stops but Maxwell kept stuffing it like an amateur chef on Thanksgiving filling a turkey to the brim. He tossed the cash inside - actually quite heavy, considering he needed to rely on his own muscles instead of his command of the electromagnetic force - and turned around to proceed with his work.

It happened all at once when the windows above his head shattered under the heels of the FBI's HRT, rappelling inward from above. The whooping of their helicopters' blades wasn't loud enough to drown out the terrifying jingle of shattered glass cascading onto the bank's floor only to shatter into even smaller pieces.

"You yanks and your guns," Maxwell smirked. "Well! Since you're here, let's have some fun!"

Relief washed over Maxwell when he saw the dozen officers carrying their M4 assault rifles and running at him with their shiny buckles, belts, and rappel clips jingling like Christmas bells against their armor. He let most of the hostages go earlier because he didn't want to get into some boring, drawn out standoff with megaphones and negotiations and all the talk, talk, talk the constables loved so much.

He came for some action, and until his date showed up he wanted to pregame. Besides, it's not like there was some magic signal he could throw into the sky to call his date, and Maxwell wasn't sure if he could use super-hearing or something, so Maxwell would need to make a lot of noise to let his guest know the party had started without him.

"Metal body armor?" asked Maxwell with a grin. "Seriously?"

With a dozen guns trained at him, Maxwell could barely suppress his grin while the HRT surrounded him. Oh, who was he kidding? Maxwell had *no* poker face and he knew it.

Without moving, Maxwell suddenly popped open a fist and extended his fingers, putting on a little show with his hands. Like a conductor, he waived his hands into the air and the HRT took flight. The officers now dangled in the air, quivering like marionette dolls as Maxwell's will traveled through the air and grabbed their assault rifles. He order the metal in the guns to leap from their owners' hands and turn around on them. Each agent now stared down the barrel of his own gun.

Maxwell noticed one of the guns was actually a tactical shotgun, and he got a fun idea. He slowly moved his wrist with a delicate motion, entirely unnecessary but kind of fun to be honest, and pulled an agent toward him along with the shotgun.

Maxwell walked up to the agent, still as a statue, a will of steel. This had been so much more fun than Maxwell had expected, though he was getting impatient waiting for his date. He ached with excitement and needed to get a little out of his system, and while the HRT were no challenge at all they might provide some amusement to kill the time (pun intended).

"Beg," said Maxwell, staring at the agent. The agent tried his best to turn his head to the side, but Maxwell's command over the metal in his helmet, goggles, and even the fillings in his teeth kept the man's head locked in place. "I want to hear you beg for me."

The agent's silence excited Maxwell even more. The challenge of the thing made it worth doing; the genuine terror as they begged for their lives made it good. If they just pretended Maxwell could tell.

CHK-CHK! The shotgun yelled as Maxwell's power cocked the gun. Now the officer started to sweat. He sneered a little to try to cover his fear, and frankly he wanted to cry. Years of training and experience couldn't prepare the agent for the fright he felt for a foe who turned the very laws of physics upside down.

Maxwell glared, wondering how far the agent would take this, wondering if he'd actually have to blow this yank's head clean off, before he heard the young voice behind him. Maxwell couldn't begin to articulate the excitement he felt when he heard it. It was like seeing your food headed toward you at a restaurant when you were really hungry. And, just as he'd expected, his date dressed to impress.

The Magnificent had arrived.

Magnificent

The Official Novelization

By Carmelo G. Chimera

Dedications

To anyone who ever dreamed of growing up to be a superhero.

And to Christine Kelley, my first fan.

-Carmelo

A novel from Chimera's Comics

www.chimerascomics.com

www.carmelochimera.com

ISBN: 978-0997577617 ISBN-10: 0997577614

Chimera's Comics® is a trademark of Carmelo G. Chimera. First paperback printing: March 2018. Originally published as a graphic novel.

Cover art by Steven Brown. Cover colors by Matthew Waite. Cover design by Carmelo Chimera.

10 9 8 7 6 5 4 3 2 1

Prologue

For something so beautiful, the Mona Lisa lived a hard life. To see her subtle color pallet and her enchanting gaze, you'd never imagine she'd suffered all kinds of attacks - from acid, to stones, to spray-paint. In a strange way, the Mona Lisa's beauty made her a target.

The worst came during the two years she spent in the custody of the thief Vincenzo Peruggia - who literally slipped her under his coat and walked out the front door with her. Still, even he honored the painting's majesty. They say imitation is the highest form of flattery — but maybe it's theft. In any case, for the last 60 years or so, she had been shielded by bulletproof glass. And there she should remain, protected and treasured, forever.

Which is why it was so alarming when she found herself inside the flat of Maxwell Edison. Unlike Peruggia, Maxwell had not stolen the painting for its place in Italian history, nor its fame amongst art scholars, and certainly not for its monetary value. No, Maxwell stole the Mona Lisa for the same reason he did anything else: because he felt like it. He thought the painting actually quite ugly, but other people valued it and called it beautiful and so he had to have it.

As usual, Maxwell awoke at noon to traipse by priceless works of art and ancient treasures, in front of one of the most beautiful urban views on the face of the planet Earth, with a television big and bright enough to make a screen in Times Square blush, to enjoy his cereal and watch some cartoons.

Maxwell brushed passed the *Mona Lisa*, totally ignorant of the many injustices she'd suffered through the years, and plopped down in his leather Swedish massage chair. The lean black Londoner sat back and kicked his feet up onto the antique cherry wood coffee table in front of him, his heels resting on a copy of *Action Comics* #1, the most valuable comic book of all time. As he wiggled into a more comfortable position, his feet tore the cover of the million-dollar magazine. Oh well. Maxwell had already finished reading it.

Maxwell spilled some of his Fruity Hoops cereal onto his purple robe when he reached for his remote control, precariously perched atop the Maltese Falcon on his side table. Maxwell flicked a switch and his telly - really a small movie theater - glowed to life. Behind the television, the bay windows of Maxwell's flat gave a commanding view of the London skyline.

Maxwell yawned while he flipped through the channels before hitting the news, and took a big spoonful from the cereal bowl he held in his arms. Milk dribbled down the corner of his lip.

"…authorities still on the hunt for the serial art thief plaguing Europe's finest museums," said the pretty newscaster. If she hadn't been talking about Maxwell, he wouldn't have been able to pay attention to her words - not while she was showing off such fair skin, curly brown hair, and bright blue eyes.

"Experts say the thief's motives are unclear, because the uniqueness of each stolen piece would make it nearly impossible to sell on the black market without betraying the thief's identity," said the gorgeous news anchor.

Maxwell ran a hand through his frizzled hair. The static electricity constantly running through his body even at rest made his hair stand on end.

Maxwell felt bored, as he had for years. He wanted for nothing - if he needed a car he would take it. If he wanted a steak he would take it. If he wanted the company of a woman (or a man) he would take that too. But as Thomas Payne once wrote, "what we acquire too cheaply we esteem too lightly." And so none of these things in Maxwell's life brought him any pleasure. Money, sex, food - all of it was truly worthless. With his powers he could have whatever he wanted, whenever he wanted it, and no one could stop him. So there was nothing really worth having.

But good things come to he who waits. The next news story brought Maxwell something he had no idea he'd been looking for.

"From the United States, the miraculous intervention of a young boy saved the lives of almost a half dozen civilians and two firemen trapped in a burning apartment building on Chicago's Southside," said the newscaster. The ticker at the bottom read "Southside Superhuman Saves Lives."

Maxwell leaned forward, on the edge of his seat now while the news station switched from showing the anchor to interview footage of a police officer. The news identified him as Detective Abraham Bentley.

"At first we told him to get lost," said the detective to the unseen news correspondent. "We thought it was a joke at best; I mean, he was wearing spray painted boots. We had no idea what he would do next."

The news anchor's voice cut in again: "To viewers at home, we caution you not to panic at what you are about to see."

Maxwell's eyes went wide while he rubbed his hand along the goatee growing around his chin. He watched as the burning apartment complex collapsed inward, spewing dust and smoke into the air.

"Oh my god, he's still *in there*!" screamed a voice from the crowd.

"Jesus, stay *back!*" yelled another.

There was a moment of silence after the dust settled, and the camera held its focus on the fallen rock.

Suddenly, the rock exploded outward. Maxwell shot back in his seat, as if he himself had been thrown by the force. And there, climbing out of the wreckage, was the Magnificent.

Maxwell felt the voltage swell inside of him. He knew from the second he saw the teenage super-hero this would be the love of his life. The camera tried to chase after him to get a better look at the red-and-blue superhero, his homemade costume covered in soot and debris, before the boy shot off *into to the sky*, his cape flapping in the wind as he flew high above the crowds.

Maxwell hadn't felt anything like this in years. He felt uncomfortable…but it was *so* pleasing. This feeling was desire. Wanting is such a pleasurable feeling; it gives one purpose, it gives one something to look forward to. It's the why of all things. And it was something Maxwell hadn't felt in so long. But when he looked at the Magnificent, Maxwell knew what he wanted.

"No, it's not a hoax," Maxwell heard the voice of Detective Bentley saying. "He told us to call him 'the Magnificent.' For a reason, too. I saw him leave the ground right in front of me. And even if it were some illusion...I don't know how he could have survived the building collapsing on him.

"He's a hero!" said another voice, a fireman. "We were trapped in there, and he rushed in - no regard for his own life. He held up the roof when it started to cave in, told us all to get out!"

Maxwell already heard everything he needed to know. Already he'd leapt out of his chair, his bowl of cereal on the ground, spilt milk running across the floor and toward the unfortunately placed *Mona Lisa*.

Maxwell didn't even dress. He'd find clothes on the way. He walked out of the front door of his flat in his purple robe and slippers. Maxwell gestured backward with his hands without looking. He didn't notice the sound anymore, but there was the faint crackle of static electricity as Maxwell's designer purple sunglasses levitated across the room and into his waiting hand. He didn't close the door behind him, because Maxwell knew he'd never return. If he did ever return, he'd simply get another apartment. But if the Magnificent lived in Chicago, then *that's* where Maxwell would be.

By the time Maxwell got to the airport, the clock nearly struck midnight. Maxwell got a pretty early start to the day (for Maxwell), but now it was pretty late. He'd stopped off at Beyond Retro for a new pair of jeans he'd taken from some hipster; he swung by Joan's flat for one last leg-over; and he grabbed one last pint with the droogs before heading to Heathrow.

Maxwell couldn't stop thinking about the Magnificent the whole way. He shook with anticipation thinking about the awesome battle waiting for him. They could wreck a whole building - maybe a whole city block together! Powerful, passionate, and explosive - everything Maxwell's life had been missing ever since he manifested his incredible superpowers.

The airport looked beautiful at night. Maxwell admired the curvature of the building, glowing blue under the purple haze of the midnight sky. The airport hired more security than it used to; no one remembered the old days when everyone wore their Sunday's best to the airport. No, now if you wanted within 50 feet of the gate you got groped, prodded, and interrogated.

Still, Maxwell had been doing this a long time. The metal detectors were useless when he walked through them; the security cameras would fritz out at his mental command; and since all the locks which weren't magnetic were still made of metal, he could come and go as he pleased.

The hardest part - the one Maxwell still hadn't figured out - was how to get passed the airline employee at the gate. You must show a boarding pass, and your ID. Maxwell possessed neither. He probably could've bought a ticket - even though he didn't have any money, it would've been easy to procure a credit card. But he never bothered with details like those.

He counted on his ability to charm anyone he met in order to bypass the sentinel of security standing between him and his flight to Chicago. In fact, Maxwell probably could have charmed the airline attendant - if he hadn't been so distracted by how fit she was. He got sidetracked chatting her up only for security to ironically escort him away.

Maxwell's cock-up with the airline employee meant he would need a new plan, so as soon as he was out of sight of the gate he gave both security guards a little taze at the base of their skulls with a sharp CRACK as the electric-purple energy erupted from his finger tips. Both of the guards dropped, still alive though - no point in making a fuss - as surely as if Maxwell used a stun gun. A wave of Maxwell's hands opened a few more doors and led him out to the tarmac.

He left another tazer victim tied up behind a dumpster and put the man's stylish green jumpsuit on. With his expert disguise as a baggage handler, Maxwell stepped out into the crisp night air, the roaring of jet engines deafening as he approached his target. He grabbed a few pieces of luggage off the cart, walked right into the baggage claim area of the plane, and hunkered down for a long flight. As the cargo bay doors closed and the last of the light was blotted out, Maxwell felt pretty knackered from such a long day and closed his eyes for an even longer nap.

Maxwell whistled his favorite tune as he strolled into the large corner building, its old-fashioned mason work facade a stark contrast to the white, polished curves of Heathrow. Inside, the bank had a modern aesthetic - high ceilings, rich maroon wood, and a stylish beige floor. Maxwell admired the ornate gold trim surrounding the epicenter of the bank while he strolled toward the tellers. He swaggered passed rows of cubicles where bankers sat; passed the bank of elevators which led to the upper offices; and finally up to the teller counter.

He couldn't help but turn a head at the first skirt he saw though, and gave her a wink. Maxwell couldn't resist himself - even though he knew he didn't have any time for a slap and tickle today. No, he'd come to make a withdrawal of something much more fulfilling.

"'Ello love," said Maxwell as he approached a short, silver-haired old woman behind the teller counter. "I'm here to rob the bank."

"Good morning, sir," said the woman, counting up a last stack of cash and only half paying attention to Maxwell. His stylish leather jacket with its purple trim and gray patches made him look respectable but fashionable, and the French-styled red and white striped shirt underneath spoke to how bold he was.

Despite his conspicuous garb, the teller didn't pay much attention to Maxwell, which he of course hated. Her simple smile reflected in his purple-framed sunglasses.

"Do you have an account, sir?" asked the old woman. The name tag affixed to her forest-green cardigan read "Esther."

"No, I don't - that's why I'm robbing this bank," said Maxwell. "Like, right now."

"Are you interested in opening an account?" said Esther from behind her half-moon reading glasses.

"I...no," said Maxwell. "I just wanted…"

"Well, sir if you don't have an account and you don't want to open one I'm afraid I'm going to have to ask you to leave," Esther said.

"Is there a problem here?" asked a pudgy man in a sharply pressed gray three-piece suit, his gold cufflinks glistening in the building's warm overhead lighting. The links matched his gold tie bar, and accentuated his Winchester-style dress shirt. His triple chin and shiny bald head showed this middle-aged bank manager's world revolved around not health, but finances.

"Mr. Goldstein, this gentleman here may need the assistance of a banker," said Esther.

Maxwell removed his shiny purple sunglasses and rubbed the bridge of his nose. "No, I don't need a banker," he said. "How much more clear can I be? Is it the accent? I'm trying to rob the bank. No, I *am* robbing the bank. So, please - call the constables or whomever, chop chop please."

"Sir, I think it's time you leave," said Goldstein. "We thank you for your business." Goldstein gave a wave to someone Maxwell couldn't see.

He'd come so far, and now he was positively gobsmacked. How did Maxwell's plan turn out to be such a damp squib? Should he have brought a ski mask? A gun? He didn't need or want either, but it seemed like a prop or two would've helped get the kerfuffle going.

"Thank you, Stan," said the bank manager as a security guard approached Maxwell.

"Come with me, sir," said an old man's voice. Maxwell turned around and was almost insulted to see the security guard. An old man - probably 92 years old, it would seem - with thick square glasses, and a thicker white mustache. He wore a big smile, wrinkles on every inch of his face, and thin silver hair. He reached out a thin arm to gesture at Maxwell. "Let's go, true believer."

Enough was enough. This wanker bank manager and his rent a cop would never create the kind of scene Maxwell needed to attract the Magnificent. The whole point of robbing this bloody bank was to make a big fuss, maybe get some of Chicago's finest to the bank so Maxwell could give them a good show, and get the super-hero here.

Maxwell had been positively aching for a fight once he saw the young hero on the news. What else was there for the man who had everything? Money, cars, none of it mattered because it came and went so easily. But this? This was his life's purpose. People with super-powers fight each other. That's the point. And it'd been so long since he'd had a real fight he'd almost forgotten how good it felt.

Maxwell Edison lost his patience. "Oh bloody hell," he said, raising a hand. Purple electric-static energy began to crackle between his fingers. The light grew brighter and brighter. Finally, with a thunderous boom, lightning arced from the palm of his hand and straight into the guard.

The whole bank seemed to flash with the strobing light of Maxwell's eruption. Esther shrieked, but you wouldn't have heard it over the sound of popping electricity shooting from Maxwell's hands. Stan the security guard seemed to glow, and you could nearly make out the black silhouette of his skeleton. The smell of burning hair and flesh grew stronger, but the attack happened so fast Stan was already incinerated before he could smell it.

Maxwell turned back to look at Esther and Goldstein with a smile. "Now," said Maxwell. "About my withdrawal…"

Chapter 1
Paved With Good Intentions

12 hours After the Event. Blackstone Bravo Base. Location Unknown.

The enormous structure sat in the middle of nowhere. Miles of sand and rock surrounded the glass and steel facility in every direction. The lack of light pollution betrayed how far it was from any civilization. In fact, an infinity of stars would have blanketed the dark heavens above, if the facility itself didn't glow like a Christmas tree. If you could fly back a ways into the sky, you might see further beyond there some forested areas formed a natural barrier; and even further, some mountainous terrain.

A single dirt road approached the gates of the facility, where a loan monolithic checkpoint cleared every vehicle going in or coming out. The huge amount of windows meant one could see into a good portion of the facility, which might seem odd given the secret nature of the base. But the location itself was so closely guarded no one would ever get close enough to look through those windows and live to tell the tale. Besides, they hid all of the really scary stuff underground.

The security present there gave little doubt Bravo Base served a military function. Roving sentries armed with automatic weapons and full body armor would have given it away alone, but the subtler signs stood out too - like automated machine turrets. The building's purpose made its design all the more bizarre, because the United States government had neither the funds nor the sense of style to build this futuristic,

Hollywood version of a military base. That meant one thing: private money.

Bravo Base provided the not-for-the-public headquarters of Blackstone Security, Inc. Blackstone billed itself as a private security contractor - a euphemism for mercenaries.

Very gradually, a slow and steady rumble ripped apart the quiet around Blackstone's Bravo Base. The whooping of helicopter blades made enough noise, but three of them combined was absolutely deafening. The sound grew louder and louder as the trio of jet-black, unmarked, stealth helicopters approached the base. The enormous firepower those helicopters concealed betrayed the true purpose of the so-called "search and rescue" unit.

"Bravo Base, this is Search and Rescue 1," crackled a voice over the radio. "Priority access code Sierra-117."

"Roger that," replied command and control inside Bravo base. "Good to hear from you, Commander Bottari."

"Bravo Base, my EMTs better be ready when we touch down," said Field Commander Alfio Bottari from the shotgun seat of the lead helicopter. "We have a high value acquisition here and he doesn't look good."

Bottari looked over his shoulder to see their "patient." The burns obscured most of the boy, but anyone who'd seen the news in the last two years would recognize the melted remains of his red-and-blue bodysuit and charred, tattered red cape.

"Roger that, Commander," came the disembodied voice of Bravo Base command and control over the radio. "Dr. Gray is standing by with a team."

The landing went fast, as Commander Bottari had done this many times. His soldiers flooded out of the his escort helicopters to secure a perimeter around the landing site, as his medics pulled the patient out of the lead helicopter. Four guards escorted the gurney with their guns aimed at the translucent plastic tent keeping the patient quarantined. Bravo Base's security kept it safe from danger, but transporting a high value target - that is to say, *patient* - brought all kinds of fresh dangers to their door. And, given the base's secrecy, rarely did the base's security have to mobilize in its own defense.

Outside, no markings indicated the identity of the silver and glass monolithic Bravo Base. But inside, Blackstone branded every door, weapon, and piece of armor with its logo. A set of double doors displayed the company's motto, *Semper Vigilans*, circling the distinctive black obelisk logo constantly reminded every soldier, doctor, and janitor of who they worked for.

Those double doors burst open now, as the EMTs butted in and around the soldiers, racing the gurney under the fluorescent glow of the impossibly long hallway. The EMTs all wore radioactive hazmat suits.

"Get him straight into containment, we've got to get him secured and stabilized so we can decontaminate," said a voice from inside one of the bright yellow Hazmat suits. "We're going to have to debride these burns."

The Doctor stopped suddenly when he felt a hand grasp his shoulder. He looked down to see the tactical glove, but he didn't have to turn around to know it belonged to Commander Bottari.

"We have been waiting for this chance for *years*," said the Italian Commander with his thick Brooklyn accent. "Do *not* lose this patient, Dr. Gray."

"I know what I'm doing, *Alfio*," said Dr. Gray, brushing his hand aside. "Now get to decontamination! There's radiation everywhere and the geiger counters are off the charts!

Commander Bottari couldn't get through decontamination fast enough. He needed to get to observation ASAP so he could observe his quarry. His heavy body armor and decontamination suit kept him slow. He stripped down completely and showered off, while hazmat personnel scrubbed his lean, muscular build down with rough, coarse bristles.

He tossed on a Blackstone sweatshirt and cargo pants he kept in his locker, let the doctors take a quick blood sample, and even popped some pills to prevent radiation poisoning and queasiness given how close he'd been to the fallout.

It took nearly an hour to jump through all the protocols and hoops Blackstone utilized for decontamination before Commander Bottari was in the observation room, glaring down at the team of doctors working on his prey. They cut off the remains of the patient's uniform. So many of the doctors surrounded him Bottari could barely see anything. But the overhead cameras pointing down from the ceilings could see over the shoulders of all the doctors in the glistening white operating room, and so Bottari turned to the high-definition monitors hanging in the room around him to see the boy.

Bottari had been looking for his chance at this target for years. The best minds at Blackstone couldn't figure out how to hurt him or stop him, so Blackstone never launched any real operation to take him down. Still, the Commander met the Magnificent on a few occasions, and every time he stifled the nearly overwhelming urge to take his chances and put one right between the smug little bastard's eyes.

Blackstone's current operation preoccupied them for the better part of a year, as the private security contractor devoted unimaginable resources to the planning and execution of its biggest single mission to date. It had been a tremendous success - but despite the success and difficulty of the operation, everyone at the company really celebrated the Magnificent's capture. Acquiring the Magnificent was just a lucky coincidence - their primary operation left the would-be teenage super-hero vulnerable to capture. But Bottari would never let an opportunity like this one slip by. His quick-thinking allowed Blackstone to capitalize on the chance to bring the freak in once and for all.

"Where did you find him?" said a deep, powerful voice from behind the Commander. Bottari possessed nerves of steel, but the presence of the General always left the hair on the back of his neck standing on end.

"About three miles from ground zero," said the Commander, never taking his eyes off the screens showing the Magnificent, or his vitals, or his dossier. "He skid the whole way…he left a crater. Like a long trail right in the ground."

16

"His durability is tremendous," said the General, stepping up next to the Commander. The Commander was an impressive physical specimen - tan, with dark hair and eyes, a trim swimmer's build and a chiseled jaw. A distinctive scar above his left eye split his eyebrow in two. But for all the character and force the Commander possessed, the General completely dwarfed him.

The General's height and broad shoulders gave him an imposing presence even before his deep, smokey voice uttered a single word. The lines on his leathery face told the story of many battles, trials, and triumphs from long, long ago. His once blue eyes dulled and grayed over the years, and those same years of furrowing his brow gave him a near permanent scowl.

"Excellent work, Alfio," said the General to his young protege. "We might have missed this window if not for your keen insight."

"Thank you, sir," said the Commander. "I couldn't sit by and watch an opportunity like this one slip by."

The General stepped closer to the biggest monitor, a close-up on the Magnificent's eyes. "You make sure Dr. Gray keeps him isolated," said the General of Blackstone. "I can't have him poisoning any of my men."

Down in the operating room, Adam was barely conscious. He kept writhing and screaming, but the pain was so blinding he barely knew where he was. All the doctors around him made him think he this could be a real hospital. But under the blinding bright lights of the operating room, he could just barely make out the silhouette of the General and the

Commander in the observation room above. If they were military, then Adam was in serious trouble. But the lights were so blinding…and the anesthetics made everything fuzzier…and the lights were so bright.

8 Years Until the Event. A playground. Suburbs of Chicago, Illinois.

Adam Garfield held up his pudgy hand to block his eyes from the sun's endless brightness. No clouds covered the crystal clear sky, matching the child's eyes. Despite the blinding light, Adam could still hear his classmates calling out teams for kickball.

"We'll take Jimmy!" shouted Brendan Lane, a tall child with the color of a parking cone. He wore a baseball cap to protect his delicate pale skin from the sun, even though his cheeks already swam through a sea of freckles. Adam secretly hoped Brendan would pick him for the team so Adam could impress Brendan. Maybe then the red-haired child wouldn't pick on Adam so much.

"And we'll take Erika," said the other captain, a short Mexican boy Adam didn't recognize. He must've gone to one of the private schools nearby.

With Erika's draft onto the kickball team, Adam was all that was left. But Brendan turned around and waived for his team to head over to the diamond across the freshly cut green grass of the suburban playground.

"What about me?" asked Adam, jogging to keep up, his weight slowing him down.

Brendan laughs. "Ha! Get lost, Adam."

"Come on," said Adam. "I brought the ball!"

"Adam, we actually need players who can run the bases," said Erika. "With you playing we'll be here all day!"

"I'm fast enough!" said Adam as the other children laughed, running away.

Erika looked back at Adam to taunt him when she tripped on the curb. She let out a yelp as she fell hard, skinning her knee.

Adam jogged over to the cute little girl as fast as he could, and under her long brown hair he could see tears rolling down her cheek and dripping off onto her grape colored t-shirt.

"Are you alright?" Adam asked. She looked up and saw him, the bright sun behind his head and in her eyes. It almost looked like his red t-shirt was glowing. Now she was crying not because of her skinned knee, but because of embarrassment for making fun of the only child to come back for her.

Suddenly, Adam jerked as the kickball slammed into the side of his face. He screamed as the rubber smacked his cheek, leaving marks as red as a cherry all over as the texture of the ball imprinted his face.

Adam hit the ground next to Erika, and he looked up to see Brendan laughing at him.

"Don't let him touch you, Erika!" called Brendan.

Erika was already up and running away. "Yuck, keep your cooties away from me!" Erika yelled as she ran toward Brendan with the others on the kickball field.

Adam sat up, hot tears rolling down his cheeks as he whimpered, "I was only trying to help…"

Chapter 2
Carpe Diem

1 Month After the Event. Blackstone Bravo Base. Location unknown.

The Magnificent didn't look like he could live up to his name right now. Strapped onto a table which rotated up to keep him in standing position, bandages covered much of the skin the explosion burned away. Nearly hairless and generally scarred over, one would never know this burn patient had once been a charming, handsome, and impossibly powerful superhuman.

The General sat around a conference table in the observation room, the tele-screens giving a few angles of the prisoner, and displaying key portions of his dossier alongside his vital signs. Around the mammoth mahogany conference table sat Commander Bottari, along with the nearly-bald Dr. Asher Gray and the pale, creepy Professor Werner Shapovalov.

"Dr. Gray, are you going to be able to learn anything from the autopsy?" asked the General, glaring across the table at Dr. Gray. The Doctor used to have passion and energy, but now all he felt was weary. Thin whisps of black hair still hung from his shiny dome-like head, but those only made him look older. Dr. Gray would have looked younger if he'd been completely bald, but he'd been too busy to shave his head. Ironically, he did keep his goatee trimmed.

"Sir, autopsies are for the deceased," said Dr. Gray. "You mean biopsy?"

"I meant what I said," the General growled back. The Doctor recoiled slightly, slinking back in his white lab coat.

"We can dissect his organs if we have to, General," said Doctor Gray, "but there's no guarantees. We have to keep him sedated so he can't use his powers - but we can't study them if we shut them off. I don't think we can do this without his cooperation. If he would work with us —"

"*For* us, Doctor," Commander Bottari interrupted. He now wore his standard-issue Blackstone bodysuit. Kevlar weave in the jacket kept him protected and mobile, and his steel-toed boots laced up and over his combat cargo pants provided comfort and force when necessary. His fingerless tactical gloves ensured optimum protection while maintaining dexterity, and the vision-enhancing goggles he kept on his head meant the Commander could jump into action at a moment's notice. Normally he might not be so decked out for a meeting at the base, but if the Magnificent gave them any trouble the Commander wanted to stay ready to execute his "containment" plan without warning.

"Hmm," agreed the General, nodding. "it looks like we don't have much choice other than to get him to cooperate, but if push comes to shove we need to have another option."

"Have you considered ze psychoanalytical approach?" inquired Professor Shapovalov. The only thing whiter than the Professor's skin was his hair. Barely anyone could understand the Professor's thick accent, but his tone combined with the lifeless look in his eyes left no doubt as to his meaning. "Perhaps ze subject could be properly motivated with the application of psychological pressure?"

"I'd love nothing more than to put the squeeze on this kid," said the General. "A little discipline is exactly what this little brat needs. But we can't get personal until we know who he really is."

Commander Bottari looked at Dr. Gray again. "Doctor, we have the best facial recognition software in the world. In *the world*. Why hasn't your team been able to identify him yet?"

"Alfio, the software's no good if we have nothing to cross-reference it with," said the Doctor. "We can't find his face because…well, he doesn't have one. He's nobody. That's why he never wore a mask."

"What do you mean, no one?" asked the General.

"I mean, he may not even have a driver's license!" exclaimed the exasperated Doctor. "There's no passports, no criminal record - nowhere we could get a photo from."

"Then we'll have to use high school yearbooks," replied the General impatiently.

"Sir, even if every company kept digital files of their yearbooks, it would take years to go through every single one in the country. And some of them may only exist as hard copies; we'd have to scan those into the program."

"Do it," snapped the General. "We need something to use against him."

Down in the room, Adam tested his restraints. He clenched his fist, felt his wrist pulse against the leather straps, and gave a tug. They barely budged, and even this light exertion left Adam's arm feeling weak and nearly numb. A haze filled Adam's thoughts, but he got a better idea of the room around him now. A large bright spotlight shone on him in the middle of an otherwise dark room. It might be the same operating room from his intake, but the doctors gave him so much anesthesia he only retained a vague recollection. In fact, Adam had no idea how much time passed since the blast, and since these doctors got ahold of him.

He thought he remembered a sterile room, white as snow; instead, this room looked like a layer of grime covered every surface. Weird stains on the tiles and grout around Adam circled a few drains on the floor. Adam wondered about the stains, and where they'd come from, or who they'd come from - until the groan of metal interrupted his muddled thoughts. A door opened.

A bright line pierced the darkened room, and an imposing silhouette stood tall in the frame, high above Adam's head. The shadow spoke: "You won't be able to use your abilities here."

The shape started to walk, disappearing into the darkness, followed in by an entourage of other shadows. Adam heard footsteps as the silhouette and his crew descended the staircase.

"We've got you on enough dope to keep an elephant down, so don't bother trying to escape," came the disembodied voice of the dark figure.

Then, the shadow returned, approaching Adam, level with him now. As the shadow entered the light, Adam saw the menacing frame of the General. Dr. Gray, Professor Shapavolov, and Commander Bottari all surrounded Adam. Other technicians began to hustle about, plugging in machines and hooking Adam up to IVs, electrodes, and other equipment. But when the General spoke, all the technicians slowed just a little bit.

"You weren't fast enough," said the General. "It was a brave thing you did, going after the nuke alone. But I want you to know you failed."

Adam hardly had the strength to speak, and the shock of this news nearly stopped his heart cold. Since his captivity he'd nearly forgotten about the explosion, the incredible force of the shockwave throwing him backward, the heat...And now the only warmth Adam felt was the heat of a tear rolling down his cheek.

"Millions of people are dead. Because of you," said the General.

Now, the old veteran stepped in close. He rested a weathered hand on Adam's shoulder. "But I admire your bravery, son. Truly. You have great potential. And I want to see your best."

The General turned away, and grabbed a tablet from an assistant. The glowing screen displayed a dossier on the Magnificent, and as the General swiped different news clippings of the young hero flashed by.

"*The Magnificent*," the General said mockingly. "Quite a bold claim to make. But you know what? You were actually pretty impressive sometimes. The fire, Maxwell Edison...really. You have a lot of potential."

Now, the General turned and spoke more sternly (as if that were possible). "But you're always going it alone. Just like you'd think a super-hero should. Predictable. But pathetic. It's time to grow up."

The General stepped in close again. Uncomfortably close.

"We knew exactly where that missile was the entire time. If you worked with us, you could've caught it and thrown it into orbit. But you can't do this alone anymore."

The General's voice softened, and he put his hand under Adam's chin to tilt his head upward. "I want to see you make it right. I want to see you become a *real* man. Work with me, son. Help me. We can train you, make you more powerful than ever before. Let us measure your abilities, and tell us all about them. We can reproduce your powers, give them to an army. And you'll be the first. Together, we'll change the world."

Adam remained silent. He glared back at the General. A fog still covered his thoughts, and now all this, all at once. What was going on? Who was this General? These guys didn't look like government. But they certainly possessed money and equipment. And guns. What did they want? What did they know about the nuke? And how much did they know about Adam?

The General grew impatient. Fast. Rage filled his eyes even though his face remained stoic. With a whisper he said, "I'm going to take what you've got, one way or another. The scientists tell me we need your cooperation. But I don't care if it takes them years - I will get all of your secrets."

Adam shook as the technicians continued their work, and the General made his way up the stairs and toward the light of the still ajar door above Adam's head. The ceilings in this room must have been towering for there to be an entrance from a second story.

"Conduct your experiments, Doctor," the General called down from the top of the stairs. "Let me know when you've got something. And when you're done, the Professor will start administering the hyoscine pentathol with intermittent electrical shocks. Keep pushing the voltage - you can take it, can't you?"

The General stopped at the top of the stairs, and leaned over the railing. "When you're ready to save the world, son, just let me know."

The General stepped through the door and it slammed shut. Darkness.

Two Years Until the Event. Hyde Park, Chicago, Illinois.

The brave fireman saw only darkness before him as he lead a group of survivors away from an inferno — only to have a portion of the ceiling collapse in front of him. The blind leading the blind. Dust and soot shot up into the air as the support beams of the ceiling caved in, slamming into the ground with a giant crash.

The fireman looked back, barely able to see through his mask. Behind him, another firefighter held a scared child in his arms, while one tenant helped his neighbor, an old man whose leg was injured. These poor folks, along with another child and his mother, had been trapped by the blaze in their Southside Chicago apartment building, unable to leave the basement at all.

The firemen fought their way down while their brothers-in-arms cleared some of the upper floors, but the fire accelerated too quickly and now they were trapped. The unfinished concrete floor of the basement meant they couldn't go any further down. This firetrap of a building, with its outdated wiring and the amateur repair jobs to its gas pipes and furnace, would likely become a tomb for these would-be survivors.

Outside the police cordoned off a large area. A single news van showed up, but more were on the way, given anyone could see the smoke from this blaze for miles in any direction. But most of the gawkers held up their smartphones and digital cameras, their iPods and their Galaxies, their Fulcrum Links or their Windows Phones. Between them, they filmed plenty of footage and flooded social media with it — shots of burn victims in ambulances, several firetrucks, and the frantic hustle and bustle of police and EMTs.

"Back, back!" screamed one officer in uniform, waving his arms wildly to keep the gawkers away from the flames and debris filling the atmosphere around the fire. Hyde Park was a strange neighborhood - parts full of money and million dollar brownstones, while sometimes only a block over the streets were lined with firetraps and condemned buildings riddled with bullet-holes from gang violence.

The crowd seemed to part in front of the uniformed officer as a strange figure walked toward him. No doubt, the young boy's outfit inspired the crowd's reaction.

He couldn't have been more than 15, maybe 16, and wore a blue t-shirt with a bright red "m" on the chest. It looked screen-printed. He wore red shorts over his white pants, tucked into combat boots the officer swore the boy spray-painted red to match. No, this boy had *for sure* spray painted his combat boots. If that wasn't enough, the pudgy teenager also wore a four-foot red cape, wrapped around his neck.

The boy surprised the officer for a moment despite the commotion of the flaming apartment building less than a football field behind him. He grew more distracted as the young boy approached him, and indeed even started to speak.

"Look!" someone yelled in the crowd, holding up their Link to get a good shot of the boy. The all-purpose mobile device held a better camera than any other mobile, and actually got a pretty decent look at the boy in the cape, though from the side.

"What is this?" said the officer, incredulous.

"I'm here to help, *ahem*, officer!" said the boy in his most authoritative voice. His red-gloved fists rested on his waists, striking a classic super-hero pose like those the boy looked at in comic books since before he could even read.

"Uh, right," said the officer, staring at the boy's costume. "Just take a step back and stay safe. We appreciate your…enthusiasm but the pros got this."

"But I can help you," said the boy again, a little confused.

"Look, kid -"

" ' The Magnificent', actually," said the boy, interrupting.

"Uh, Detective?" the officer called, waving over someone out of uniform. "Detective, um…we have a kid here…"

" 'The Magnificent'," the boy repeated with a proud look on his face, puffing out his chest and sticking his chin up.

"How old are you kid?" said the impatient black detective from under his thick mustache.

"I'm…I'm 15, sir."

"Listen, you can help by staying the hell back and not getting yourself hurt. We got this under control."

"Detective Bentley!" yelled another officer, a woman, running up to the duo. She addressed the plain-clothes Detective Abraham Bentley. "Detective, I just heard, everyone's clear of the building but a pair of firefighters are trapped in the basement with some civilians. They're pinned!"

"What?" Detective Bentley barked. "How many?"

"We don't know yet sir!" the Latina officer shot back, a desperate look in her eyes. "Maybe three or four, we can't tell."

"I can help," the Magnificent interjected again.

"Kid, ENOUGH!" screamed Bentley, ready to walk away.

"Fine," said the Magnificent. He stuck his arms out to the side, and felt the familiar rush of air underneath him as the ground started to pull away from his feet.

The commotion in the crowd caused Bentley and the other two officers to turn around in shock. They raised their eyes, then had to tilt their heads, to see the Magnificent raise upward into the air, his cape flapping. The Magnificent was *flying*.

The red-and-blue wonder boy hung in the air above them, looking down. The sun shone bright behind his head. For a moment, he looked like an angel.

"Let me help," said the Magnificent, his voice inspired with surety and confidence as everyone gawked at his marvelous ability to defy gravity.

Bentley had no idea what to say. "Uh….ok," was all he managed to eek out.

That was all the Magnificent needed to hear. He glared at the blaze with his bright sapphire eyes, picked his target, and leaned forward. Stretching his fists out in front of him, he blasted toward the building in a blur, faster than he'd meant to, and crashed into the side of the building.

He was so eager to get inside, he messed up the landing pretty bad. He crashed into the floor and tumbled a bit, then stood. Thankfully, no one outside saw it.

The Magnificent looked around. He stood in a hallway on the first floor of the building. He'd never been this close to a fire, and now it surrounded him. He almost thought the glowing flames around him looked cool, wrapping around the building as if they were themselves alive. As he walked, he wondered if his abilities would protect him from fire - but no sooner did the thought cross his mind than the young hero started to cough. Powers or not, he needed to breathe, and soon he was hacking quite a bit. He *almost* didn't notice the corner of his cape catch fire.

But he did notice, and felt an appropriate freakout. He jumped up and down a bit, grabbing his cape and flapping. That only made it worse. He started to stomp on the cape, and it helped until his foot stomped straight through the floor, and he tripped forward. Luckily, he caught himself - just in time for a burning beam to crash through the ceiling and smash apart over his head.

The Magnificent was nearly invincible to physical harm, though, so the thunderous smash of the burning beam bruised only the ego of the young super-hero.

Suddenly, he heard it - a scream. A cry for help, from below him.

The Magnificent was vaguely aware of how cool his cape looked as he turned suddenly and darted forward to a door to the basement. With only a nudge it flew off the hinges, splintering into a hundred pieces. He'd have to be more careful or the next door he "opened" might crush an innocent civilian to death. Or leave them with more splinters than a porcupine.

At the bottom of the stairs, a barricade of burning debris blocked his way into the basement. This must be what trapped the civilians.

"Stand back!" he had the presence of mind to yell, before shouldering into the debris. The burning rubble gave way with ease to the boy's power. And the path for the civilians looked clear behind him. But despite their impending rescue, the firemen and the tenants stood still in shock to see a super-hero come to their rescue.

The Magnificent honestly enjoyed the look on their faces. "Is everyone alright?" he asked, immediately remembering why he came.

But then, he heard the shifting of wood behind him. "Come on," he said, waving everyone to the stairs.

As he tried to take the first step, the stairway itself completely collapsed inward. Now, the stairs were just a burning pile of wood, the cheap carpeting melting and filling the room with an even worse stench than before.

"What are we gonna do?!?" screamed the mother holding her child. It was almost impossible to get a good look at her now through the smoke, and even if one could see her she was covered in so much soot her closest friends may not have recognized her. And one power the Magnificent did not have was super-vision.

"Wait here!" the Magnificent called confidently, as if he had a plan. He didn't. He looked around. He could fly the survivors upstairs, but the case was narrow and he could probably only move one at a time that way. Plus, at least one of the survivors was limping with an injury. It would take too long.

The Magnificent looked at the only source of natural light, eking through a soot-covered window. The basement possessed a few small windows near the base of the building looking out into the neighborhood above. There were bars on the windows, and they didn't appear to open. They weren't windows so much as they were bricks of glass, mortared together. Even if they would open they looked far, far too small for even the children to climb out.

From the outside, the emergency servicepersons held their collective breath. The crowd had grown, and another news camera had shown up. In fact, a helicopter arrived, scrambled over from traffic reporting when the first footage of the Magnificent hit the Internet. News travelled faster than a speeding bullet these days.

All of a sudden, an enormous explosion erupted from the base of the building. Dirt and concrete shot into the air. As smoke poured from the gaping wound in the burning apartment complex, the debris settled slightly and the damage became clear: a huge pit and been made, taking a chunk out of the basement, the lawn, and the sidewalk around the building to make a hole big enough for the survivors to climb through.

The two firemen helped all of the tenants out, and everyone bolted from the building as fast as they were able.

Detective Bentley, the only person running toward the building, sprinted up to the first fireman. "Where is he?" called the veteran policeman.

"He's holding up the ceiling!" the firefighter yelled back, as loud as he could over the roaring flames. "It's incredible - he's still in there!"

The ground started to shake. Bentley's heart dropped when he felt the tremor, and he knew what was coming. He reeled, turning to see the building quaking. "No..." he whispered, filled with anger. He didn't know who or what this kid was, but Bentley had seen enough young promises and dreams dashed as officer after officer had fallen to senseless violence, accidents, and even just the incredible stress which plagued the lives of Chicago's finest. Here, another young life - bright and eager to make a difference - was about to be snuffed out before it even started.

As the tremor predicted, the building began to fold in on itself. Everyone ran from the wreckage as smoke and debris filled the air, the building collapsing and tumbling to pieces with no more structural integrity than a house of cards.

33

Deep inside, it was dark. The eery orange glow of flames provided the only light. It grew harder to see - and even harder to breathe. The Magnificent held his hands up above his head, holding the weight of most of the building on his shoulders. He huffed and puffed, trying to hold his breath before he'd gasp for air, which was only worse given all the smoke. Things started to go dark.

Two explosions in almost as many minutes made the crowd on edge as everyone tried to get as closer to the smoldering remains of the apartment building. A somber quiet came over the crowd. By now everyone on the ground and in the news choppers had heard about the hero and most had at least seen some of the footage trending online - even though he'd only made his grand entrance about 20 minutes ago now. If everyone wasn't nervous enough before, they certainly were after a third explosion came from the building.

Rocks, drywall, the remains of furniture — all of it went flying into the air with even greater force than the building came down with. And the crowd reeled at the sight of the Magnificent, any pretense of authority or power gone and replaced by the actual power he possessed as he shrugged the weight of an entire building off of his back.

The first thought going through his head wasn't pleasure at being alive, or confusion about his surroundings, or even self-consciousness about the crowd. The first thought to cross the Magnificent's mind was, *I can't believe my cape is stuck again!*

He tugged at his cape, tearing it free from the wreckage and ultimately ripping it. He felt crestfallen. But in the moment it took the Magnificent to do it, the stunned silence of the crowd was replaced by thunderous cheers and applause.

The Magnificent smiled sheepishly, turning almost as red as his cape as the crowd swarmed him, clapping and hooting and hollering like he was one of the Chicago Blackhawks after another Stanley Cup win. He almost ignored the television cameras getting a bit close for comfort, but he did come to his senses before they got too close. The Magnificent slowly rose into the air, steadily picking up speed so as not to create a sonic boom and deafen every man, woman, and child in a three-block radius. He zoomed off into the sky, but the cheers almost seemed to grow louder.

Only a few years later, those cheers became screams, and the screams were his own.

Chapter 3
The Other Shoe Drops

Four months after the Event. Blackstone Bravo Base. Location Unknown.

The General smiled as he looked at the Magnificent, panting hard and still recovering from his most recent electric shock treatment. No one had ever seen anything except electricity hurt the young hero, after that public spectacle just a few months before the big one. The General needed to administer such enhanced interrogation both to test the limits of the Magnificent's endurance and, perhaps, deduce the source of the young hero's invulnerability.

Examination was far from the only purpose. The General knew plenty of noninvasive - or at least minimally invasive - procedures which Blackstone could and in fact was currently conducting. No, the pain and truth serums, the electric shocks, the live surgeries - the General employed them to teach the boy a lesson. No matter what the scientists thought about their experiments, the General understood now the boy's cooperation would be required eventually. And the General could see the boy possessed a great power. He'd be an excellent operative. As the Magnificent he demonstrated the courage and initiative to face challenges and conquer complex obstacles.

But the boy grew too comfortable being impervious. He needed to understand the pain and the loss life would bring to him. Only then would he see the need for Blackstone's methods. Only then would he see things the General's way. The General couldn't blame the boy for being naive. He was young. But the General saw it as his responsibility to help the boy grow up.

After a few months Dr. Gray informed the General he was no closer to understanding the nature or source of the Magnificent's power. So the General felt particularly proud of himself for the new approach he'd conceived — an attempt to meet the young boy halfway. If this kid wanted to play super-hero, the General could play along. At least, long enough to show the boy what being a hero would truly require of him. That would come, with time. For now it was the time for a little more carrot and a little less stick.

With his master plan in hand, the General of Blackstone entered the laboratory where the Magnificent stood, strapped to a table, and full of so much sedative he could barely make a fist, much less fly.

"I've got something for you," said the General, waving his men in. Two soldiers approached, carrying a mannequin, and stood it up in front of the heaving and sickly young hero. The Magnificent raised his head to see a peculiar thing.

The Magnificent's eyes went wide for a moment - only a moment - and the General's confidence swelled. For the first time in maybe years, a slight smile cracked open the leathery texture of the General's lips. But his smile faded as quickly as the Magnificent's surprise, as the young hero went stoic again. Never saying a word.

It's not that the General's gift didn't impress the Magnificent. In front of him stood a super suit, not unlike the one he used to wear. Its harsh, segmented lines gave off a more tactical look, with armored shins and knees giving the suit a clearly military origin. The short-sleeved suit came with a pair of fingerless tactical gloves. The only the slightest accents of grey and silver broke up the black monochromatic armor. But, there on the chest - as prominent as ever - rested the grand and glistening crimson "M" which defined all of the Magnificent's prior wardrobes.

The General continued. "I don't need you to suffer, or to die. I need your power. It's your ticket out of here, and into a life you've always dreamed of."

He locked eyes with the Magnificent now. Decades of command, field interrogations, battle - the General could tell the boy was about to crack. He had him!

"You want to be a hero? I want the same thing. I want you to work for us, for Blackstone. You want to fight fires, pull cats out of trees? Fine. Be a hero, just like before. Only this time, you'd be paid for it. Very well. Money would never be a concern. You could have anything you wanted. I mean it.

"The only thing is, at the end of the day, you'll work for us and when we give you a mission you do it. Doing the same thing you love. Fighting bad guys, saving people. Not such a bad deal, huh?"

The Magnificent remained silent. He stared blankly at the General. The old soldier didn't understand. He saw the look in his eyes. He just offered the boy the end of his pain and torment, and the lap of luxury in exchange. Not to mention the glory. What was wrong with this kid?

No matter. He would crack if he thought about it a bit longer. The General was sure of it. So sure that, as he turned his back on the boy and headed toward the exit, the slight crack of a smile on his face grew into a twisted rictus.

He looked back to the Magnificent just before exiting the room, and the General showed the boy his toothy smile. "One day, you will talk to me," the General sneered.

One Year Until the Event. House Party. Suburbs of Chicago, Illinois.

Brendan grinned ear to ear as he wrapped his arms around Erika. He'd grown very tall. Adam barely recognized Brendan as the boy who used to throw kickballs at him on the playground - except that for all his age freckles still covered Brendan's pale skin.

The basement of this two-story suburban McMansion was crowded with Adam's classmates from school. He recognized a few people from one of his orientation classes, though most of them were strangers because Adam only took honors classes. He took all of his courses with the same twenty or so students, and none of them came to this party. Maybe it's the reason why Adam felt so uncomfortable here. But despite the crowd, across the room, Adam could see Brendan's grin as he wrapped his arms around Adam's girlfriend.

Adam grew even more uncomfortable than he already had been. He had his suspicions Erika and Brendan might have been an item at one time, but Adam wasn't the jealous type. Still, it made him nervous seeing Brendan be so liberal with Erika. And it didn't help that Adam didn't drink - he was surrounded by solo cups filled with beer, and everyone got more and more bombed. Adam already felt like an outsider all the time - the feeling became even heavier when he felt forced to keep himself in control like this. Even if he wanted to drink with his friends, he wasn't sure what would happen if he did. After all, he hadn't found an upper limit to his super-strength yet, and it required near constant control to avoid putting his foot through the floor or to open a door without tearing it off its hinges.

Between the crowd of drunken teenagers, the faint smell of skunk coming from upstairs, and Brendan's taunting smile, claustrophobia enveloped Adam. Trapped. Like an animal.

He hated to indulge his jealousy, but Erika looked uncomfortable as she wiggled out of Brendan's grip. Adam had a crush on her since they were kids. But she often hung out with a different crowd than he did. Still, he loved the dark-eyed girl-next-door enough to go out of his comfort zone for her. So Adam followed his natural instinct to rush to her rescue and walked across the room to confront Brendan.

"Brendan, enough," said Erika as she freed herself, tugging her purple sweater from Brendan's grip as he clumsily and playfully tried to paw at her. "Adam's right there."

"Oh come on," said Brendan. "That loser? Come with me…It'll be like riding a bike…"

"Brendan that's enough!" snapped Erika.

"You heard her," said Adam, approaching his lifelong tormentor. The smug look on his face and his spiky goatee suited the arrogant bully's attitude well. Before, Adam couldn't stop Brendan from picking on him. When Adam's powers manifested, he continued to let Brendan torment him because Adam feared seriously hurting him. And because he was content to know Brendan would break his own hand if he ever tried to punch Adam. Adam didn't need anyone to know it, least of all Brendan.

However, years of holding back made Adam tense. And now Erika was looking at him, telling Adam with her eyes to let Brendan have it. Maybe it was that. Maybe it was the claustrophobia. Maybe it was because Adam had been under so much pressure lately, trying to juggle classes with college applications and a part-time job at the comic book store *on top* of his super-heroic alter-ego. Whatever the reason, the anger swelled inside of him. And he could feel it. If Adam didn't know any better, he'd say he felt the room get cold around him.

"Ooo, scary!" said Brendan. "What are you gonna do? Huh? Tough guy? Come on. Show me what you got."

Adam's fist trembled as he and Brendan stared each other down.

"Show me!" Brendan shouted.

What happened next was a blur. Everything was fuzzy. Adam felt dizzy and confused. He lunged forward so fast he couldn't stop himself, and before he realized what he'd done he felt warm wetness all over his hand, dripping down his arm. The blood almost looked black as it stained Adam's cherry-red shirt. Now it was all Adam could see: red. Everything, red. He looked up, and saw Brendan's head hanging limp as Adam held him in the air above him, impaled on Adam's arm. But even though Adam had put his arm straight through Brendan and lifted him up like a doll, Brendan still sneered back at him. Grinning, his eyes taunted Adam.

Adam shook his head. It had been a fantasy, nothing more. A crowd gathered now, as Brendan and Adam continued to stare at each other. Adam wanted to do it. He really wanted to hurt Brendan. To show Brendan who really had the power. The unfairness of it all made him want to do it. Why did Brendan get to be such a jerk? Why did Brendan get to treat people however he wanted? He wasn't just a jerk - he was weak. Weaker than Adam. Why should he get to do whatever he wanted while Adam held himself back all the time?

Adam turned around and made for the door, fast. He couldn't be here anymore. He needed to get away from Brendan, to get away from the crowds, to breathe again and calm down before he lost it completely. He bumped his way passed some drunk kid in a Bears jersey, pushed passed the wood panel covered walls and up the stairs, out onto the lawn in the cool night air.

"What the hell was that?" he heard a voice shout from behind him. He turned around, and saw Erika storming out of the house behind him and stomping in her heels across a bed of posies lining the walkway to the house.

"Erika, please," said Adam, shaking his head.

"No! You could have kicked his ass! Why wouldn't you fight him?"

Adam looked at his sneakers sheepishly. He felt awful for how angry he'd gotten back there. But storming out made him look weak and that made him feel angry, too. He had done the right thing…hadn't he? From the moment he turned his back on Brendan, Adam immediately began second guessing himself. So what if he did teach Brendan a lesson? He deserved it. So what if people knew he wasn't weak? If walking away had been the right thing, why did it feel so unfulfilling?

"You fight for everyone else but me!" Erika yelled, interrupting Adam's brooding. He couldn't handle the look in her eyes. The anger, the disappointment. It was unbearable. Like her eyes were tearing straight into his heart.

"Did you know I hooked up with him?" she went on. "*Now* do you want to fight him?"

Adam stopped cold. "You…when? *Why?* So I'd hurt him?" asked Adam, his mind lost in a haze. Erika had been mad at him before. But there was something new in her voice. Beyond the volume, there was something else. Cruelty.

"So I'd know you care!" she shouted back before Adam could form another thought. "You act like this big hero! But who have you ever *really* helped? What difference have you made?"

"Erika — " Adam tried to say, more and more frustrated by how little she seemed to care about what he was trying to get out.

"*I* need you too!" she interrupted again, hammering Adam with a torrent of rage. His invulnerability meant he'd known very little physical harm - so this felt like it might kill him.

"I'm your girlfriend," Erika said. "I should be your *only* priority! But I'm not enough for your *ego*. You need *everyone* to *adore* you."

She spat the words out like venom. Adam lost it.

"You think I do this for fame?!" he shouted. He never shouted. "I could do *anything* I want. I could take anything I want! Instead, all I do is stand up for people who don't care about me!"

Erika pursed her lips - it made her look angry, but she only did it to keep from crying. It's probably why she wouldn't look him in the eye then either.

Erika tried to reach out her hand, but it was too late. Adam rose from the ground, so suddenly the gushing of air around Erika whipped her hair into her face. She felt the thunderous bellow of Adam breaking the sound barrier, like the feeling you get when fireworks go off. She couldn't see his face as he flew into the night, but he was crying. He couldn't help it.

If there had been any clouds in the sky they would have been demolished by Adam's flight. As he flew into the beautiful lavender haze from Chicago's nearby light pollution, he continued to cry. Erika had been so cruel, and thinking of her with Brendan made him feel so weak. So small. Pathetic. Like she was trying to tell Adam he wasn't special. And it hurt to think someone as special as Erika was to Adam could mean so little to someone else.

On the other hand, maybe she was right. Maybe this super-hero thing was stupid. Adam had great strength - he should act like it. It was nature after all, wasn't it? Forget nature

- don't people with power get to enjoy it? Was Adam really just a big wimp after all in his cape and boots?

The thought his life's purpose might be for nothing made him cry all the more. He squeezed his eyes tight to try and hold back the tears.

Chapter 4
You Never Forget
Your First

One Year After the Event. Blackstone Bravo Base, Location Unknown.

Painful electric shocks racing through Adam's body hurt so bad, he almost didn't notice how badly is eyes hurt from squeezing them so tight. He'd very nearly forgotten how badly it hurt to have this much current coursing through his muscles. The smell of his own skin starting to burn at the point of contact made him nauseous, but between the odor and the agonizing shockwaves pulsing through his muscles Adam was sure he'd vomit soon.

He'd vomited a couple of times during his long captivity with Blackstone - how long had it been now? He wasn't even sure. At first Adam entertained hopes of escape, then later rescue. But as the months dragged on, Adam secretly hoped next time he vomited he would choke to death and be free of his imprisonment.

Time ceased to be meaningful. The pain alone hadn't chased time away - the endless repetition of each day had. He'd awake to some terrible pain - a needle, an electric current, some injection which set his nervous system on fire. Then he'd sweat and pant and cough while they kept him alive, pumping nutrition and hydration into his body through intravenous injection. Adam couldn't count the passing of days because it became impossible to tell when he closed his eyes to sleep or to pass out from the pain his life had become. And the sedatives which kept away his precious abilities, and his freedom, kept him groggy the whole time.

If that wasn't enough to make the passage of time impossible to track, Blackstone did in fact turn time into a weapon against Adam. Blackstone employed sensory deprivation torture when they questioned Adam about his abilities. By leaving Adam blinded by a cold, metal mask while bombarding him with nightmarish sounds, minutes turned into hours turned into days.

In fact, the questioning almost hurt more than the experiments. Blackstone would alternate poking, prodding, and slicing Adam's body with doing the same thing to his mind. And just when Adam thought his body couldn't take anymore, he was almost happy to trade his sanity for a few moments without physical agony. But by the time the interrogation sessions were over, Professor Shapovalov's experiments brought a strange clarity to Adam's mind. And then the cycle would repeat.

So it could have been day 30 or day 300 when Adam opened his eyes from his latest trial. Then, he felt the creepy chill of Shapovalov's thick, Eastern European accent.

"Do you know vhat today iz, young man?" asked the mad scientist.

Adam gave the same answer he gave to every single question he was asked: he remained silent.

"Today iz ze one year anniversary of your arrival here!" the Professor continued with nearly genuine enthusiasm. "Congratulations, *kleiner junge.*"

Adam knew what this meant. The interrogations were about to begin.

"Dr. Gray continues to test your body. But I'm more interested in ze *mind*. Can you take pressure without breaking? And vhen you break, vhat vill be left?"

Adam's head hung low, staring at his feet, as always. It used to be because avoiding eye contact made it easier not to answer any questions. Then, it was because Adam no longer possessed the strength enough to keep his head high.

"I know ze secret," Shapovalov said, leaning in a bit closer, his accent making his whisper sound like a hiss. "It's not ze mind. It's ze heart."

Adam felt his body shaking. He knew what was coming. Like Pavlov's dog, he'd been conditioned. Trembling at Shapovalov's little speeches, because they always came before the interrogations.

"Man endures any how, if he has a why," the Professor explained, academically, as if talking to a classroom. "You'll break vhen you learn your suffering is *meaningless*."

He moved over to the machine.

"Are you ready, *der kleiner ausgezeichnet*?" he asked, grinning now.

Adam felt it again — the coursing, tearing sensation traveling down his nervous system and cooking his body from the inside out. Adam screamed….the bright lights on the machine sparked a menacing blue…

*****

Nine Months Until the Event. Uptown Neighborhood. Chicago, Illinois.

The blue lights of the Chicago Police cars flashed bright even in the midday sun. At least a dozen cars surrounded the bank, with at least twice as many uniformed officers spreading out to take up defensive positions and secure a perimeter. The beautiful granite facade of the building contained a sleek, modern financial institution which activated a silent alarm mere minutes before. Chicago's finest came swooping in to the rescue at the cry for help.

Now, the uniformed officers divided their attention between clearing the street of civilians and keeping an eye on the front door of the bank. It hung open limply, but the dark threshold looked ominous rather than welcoming.

The hostages inside still had their cellphones, and many shared pictures and videos to Facebook, Instagram, and Twitter. The cynic would point out how absurd these people must be to broadcast their life-and-death ordeal live to the world. But as Captain Abraham Bentley stepped out of his squad car, arriving to the scene behind all of his uniformed officers, he was still watching footage from inside the bank to study the scene. Those people were warning him, telling him what was going on inside, through their tweets and their snapchats. It was valuable intel, and those people were brave, not egoists looking for the limelight.

The footage from inside the bank shocked Bentley. Something blew the bank vault door entirely off of its hinges.

Now the vault door sat in the middle of the bank's beige marble floor, leaving a devastating crater under its enormous weight. Entire cubicles were flipped over, and the bank had been redecorated with ashen burns scorched into the walls and furniture. Most shockingly was at least two bloody smears which used to be security guards. But, there in the background of the last shot…was that…a truck?

"Uh, Captain?" asked one of the officers while Bentley kept an eye on his cellphone as he closed his squad car door behind him. "Not now!" barked Bentley.

"Captain, look!" repeated the young officer.

Bentley looked up from his phone and his eyes went wide. He didn't need the cellphone to see the gaping whole in the side of the building, big enough for an armored car to fit through. Bentley checked his phone again. It was an armored car, inside the bank, smashed right through the side of the building.

What kind of weapon could have done this? Bentley wondered. How many perps were there? Where were they? And why do this so loud, take so long? As Bentley glared at the bank, he shuddered as the only explanation occurred to him: this wasn't done by ordinary bank robbers. That like Chicago's young protector — who had been slowly earning Bentley's respect — these robbers might have strange abilities.

"Captain Bentley!" one of the officers radioed as he kept his eyes locked on the bank's doorway. "There's someone coming out!"

"Hold your positions!" barked the elder officer over the radio. "The FBI is scrambling the Hostage Rescue Team. Do NOT engage the targets unless they attack first!"

And, the targets appeared. Rather, *target*, singular. That's when Bentley knew it. He knew if this were the work of one man, then it was more than just a man.

While Bentley's heart skipped a beat, he felt a strange sensation - not fear, but confusion. The man in front of him surprised him by being strange in every way, from his dress to his gate to the excited grin on his face. He wore one of those trendy, ultra stylized European leather jackets, the kind with more pockets and zippers than it needs and even stripes on the shoulders. He looked like a punk hipster in those skinny jeans too. His purple sunglasses did nothing to disguise the man, whose distinctive fuzzy hair and giant grin would make him easy to pick out of a lineup. In fact, the flashy shades just made him stand out all the more.

Bentley reached into his car to grab a megaphone. He wanted to wait for HRT but the perp brought the fight to them. "Don't move!" he yelled through the loud speaker, as the police officers around him took up defensive positions behind their squad cars, weapons drawn and aimed at the rogue. "Put your hands in the air, and lie face down on the ground with your palms out in front of you!!"

The sigh unnerved Bentley. Even though he possessed a commanding voice and an imposing presence, the Captain secretly prayed his fear hadn't crept into his voice. The destruction inside the bank didn't scare him. Even superpowers didn't scare him - he was getting used to those from his young friend. No, it was the fact over a dozen uniformed Chicago Police Officers had weapons trained on this one man — and he couldn't have been happier to see them.

"What took you so long?" the man called out, as he slowly raised his palms in front of him. Bentley glared, waiting for the first sign of weird. But Bentley didn't need his eagle glare to see what came next. As Bentley was about to learn, this bank robber was anything but subtle.

"Guess you've all got me bang-to-rights!" called the robber with his thick English accent, hands rising in the air.

The man's hair began to stand on end as his palms started to glow and crackle with static energy dancing in between his fingers. The light got so bright it almost completely blotted out his face, awash in the brightness coming from his hands. Then, a thunderous boom tore through the air. Bentley might have mistaken the noise for gunfire from his own men, if he had a second to articulate the thought. No, the lightning shot from the bank robber's hands so quickly, Bentley ran for cover with the rest of his officers before he had time to blink.

The first bolt of electricity struck an officer square in the chest with such force it lifted him up and off of the ground and flying backward. The mailbox the officer landed on collapsed into a heap underneath of him. The second bolt tore through the front of a squad car, while two adjacent officers pivoted and tried to bolt. But they weren't fast enough, because the car's engine exploded from the energy, sending both officers flying forward and face first into the pavement.

Bentley stopped on a dime to look back at an officer as she screamed. He watched in horror as a bolt of lightning hit her from behind, and she jerked and convulsed while the crackle of electricity coursed through her body.

Bentley looked back at the bank robber. He'd stopped firing his electricity, but now he was lifting his hands slowly into the air. Bentley took cover behind the nearest squad car, though it wouldn't do him much good if the robber fired another bolt of lightning at him. If the Captain hadn't been so stunned by the carnage around him, he would've realized the robber did not intend to fight his way out, but rather to put on a show.

But the thought never crossed Captain Bentley's mind, because his thoughts were interrupted by the rumbling under his hands. He looked at the car in front of him while he rested a hand on the trunk, and saw the car shaking beneath his palm. The shaking grew more and more violent as the bank robber slowly lifted his hands. Then, the car obeyed his command, and followed his hands into the air.

Suddenly all of the police cars were flying through the air. Bentley bolted with his officers as car after car plummeted from the sky. One car smashed through the side of a building above Bentley's head, two stories up. The front of the car began to crunch inward as it slammed into the building's facade, the hood of the car buckling and folding like an accordion as the fiberglass cracked and screamed. The building's facade couldn't match the momentum and buckled in the same instant the car smashed into it. Chunks of bricks danced with shards of glass through the air and rained agony onto the sidewalk below.

The car above Bentley's head distracted him from another car, barely a hundred feet away, as it belly-flopped onto the street. A funny thing happened - the bottom of the car came to a dead stop as it hit the pavement, but the top of the car kept falling, almost cartoonishly. As the roof of the car pancaked into the bottom of the car, the middle blew outward - the glass exploded out in every direction, like flechettes tearing through the air. The doors and middle of the car popped outward as if the car had been a giant pimple, popping.

The force of this last car hitting the ground nearly knocked Bentley over. He looked around, dazed, and as he struggled to get his footing he swore he saw the bank robber wiping his hands as if to say his job was done. The bank robber turned, not even having broken a sweat, and headed back into the bank.

Bentley breathed heavily from panic. Then, he saw it: a helicopter was approaching, while a fleet of black vans and SUVs raced underneath it. Bentley's eyes went wide with terror as he realized the FBI's HRT was flying in too fast for him to warn them. But even if he could warn them he doubted the FBI would believe a single man inside the bank was about to turn all their toys and their training into a useless joke.

Maxwell Edison whistled his favorite tune, the one from which he derived his name, while he strolled back inside the bank. In no particular rush at all, Maxwell winked at a cute teller hiding behind an overturned desk, as if completely unawares of the situation and with the same casual confidence he would have displayed winking at a girl in a pub.

Maxwell obviously wasn't here for the cash - he planned to burn it all anyway, and loose the ashes on Lake Shore Drive for shiggles. But he needed to pass the time, and he thought it might help him get in character, so he strolled into the vault passed the enormous, sad metal door lying pathetically on the ground, impotent to protect its treasures after Maxwell effortlessly ripped it loose and tossed it aside with the slightest whim.

He grabbed a large brick of cash - it sort of delighted him to see the money was wrapped, packed, and taped into bundles like any other product or merchandise - and walked it over to the armored car. The car was already pretty full from its other stops but Maxwell kept stuffing it like an amateur chef on Thanksgiving filling a turkey to the brim. He tossed the cash inside - actually quite heavy, considering he needed to rely on his own muscles instead of his command of the electromagnetic force - and turned around to proceed with his work.

It happened all at once when the windows above his head shattered under the heels of the FBI's HRT, rappelling inward from above. The whooping of their helicopters' blades wasn't loud enough to drown out the terrifying jingle of shattered glass cascading onto the bank's floor only to shatter into even smaller pieces.

"You yanks and your guns," Maxwell smirked. "Well! Since you're here, let's have some fun!"

Relief washed over Maxwell when he saw the dozen officers carrying their M4 assault rifles and running at him with their shiny buckles, belts, and rappel clips jingling like Christmas bells against their armor. He let most of the hostages go earlier because he didn't want to get into some boring, drawn out standoff with megaphones and negotiations and all the talk, talk, talk the constables loved so much.

He came for some action, and until his date showed up he wanted to pregame. Besides, it's not like there was some magic signal he could throw into the sky to call his date, and Maxwell wasn't sure if he could use super-hearing or something, so Maxwell would need to make a lot of noise to let his guest know the party had started without him.

"Metal body armor?" asked Maxwell with a grin. "Seriously?"

With a dozen guns trained at him, Maxwell could barely suppress his grin while the HRT surrounded him. Oh, who was he kidding? Maxwell had *no* poker face and he knew it.

Without moving, Maxwell suddenly popped open a fist and extended his fingers, putting on a little show with his hands. Like a conductor, he waived his hands into the air and the HRT took flight. The officers now dangled in the air, quivering like marionette dolls as Maxwell's will traveled through the air and grabbed their assault rifles. He order the metal in the guns to leap from their owners' hands and turn around on them. Each agent now stared down the barrel of his own gun.

Maxwell noticed one of the guns was actually a tactical shotgun, and he got a fun idea. He slowly moved his wrist with a delicate motion, entirely unnecessary but kind of fun to be honest, and pulled an agent toward him along with the shotgun.

Maxwell walked up to the agent, still as a statue, a will of steel. This had been so much more fun than Maxwell had expected, though he was getting impatient waiting for his date. He ached with excitement and needed to get a little out of his system, and while the HRT were no challenge at all they might provide some amusement to kill the time (pun intended).

"Beg," said Maxwell, staring at the agent. The agent tried his best to turn his head to the side, but Maxwell's command over the metal in his helmet, goggles, and even the fillings in his teeth kept the man's head locked in place. "I want to hear you beg for me."

The agent's silence excited Maxwell even more. The challenge of the thing made it worth doing; the genuine terror as they begged for their lives made it good. If they just pretended Maxwell could tell.

CHK-CHK! The shotgun yelled as Maxwell's power cocked the gun. Now the officer started to sweat. He sneered a little to try to cover his fear, and frankly he wanted to cry. Years of training and experience couldn't prepare the agent for the fright he felt for a foe who turned the very laws of physics upside down.

Maxwell glared, wondering how far the agent would take this, wondering if he'd actually have to blow this yank's head clean off, before he heard the young voice behind him. Maxwell couldn't begin to articulate the excitement he felt when he heard it. It was like seeing your food headed toward you at a restaurant when you were really hungry. And, just as he'd expected, his date dressed to impress.

The Magnificent lived up to his name, a light breeze blowing through his swooping brown hair. The bright, sky blue of his sleek, two-piece costume brought out his sapphire eyes. A slight white trim along the bold, armored red "M" on his chest made the emblem pop. The young adventurer really upped the ante. His red cape flapped luxuriously behind him as he floated through a gaping window, and his bright boots made a satisfying click as they hit the ground.

"I'm so glad to see you!" Maxwell said, breaking character. Maxwell couldn't contain himself. "You look brill!" he said, noting the hero had lost weight since Maxwell had first seen him on the news. "I love your new threads!"

The Magnificent looked a little puzzled, sort of fixated on the officer hanging in front of Maxwell.

"Oh, right, sorry!" said the villain. He flicked his wrist and all of the guns clattered to the ground. The officers flew backward in every direction, crashing and clattering against the walls of the bank and tumbling down in heaps of muscle and armor on the ground.

"And where have you been all my life?" he called out to the Magnificent with a deep breath. "I can't wait to get started!"

The Magnificent heard a sudden rattling behind him as tires screeched. He could barely turn fast enough to see the armored car come to life and fly at him, driven by some phantom force. The young hero braced himself as a thunderous crash reverberated through the bank. The reinforced engine block of the car was no match for the invincible teenager, and crumpled inward. The bulletproof

58

glass of the windshield splintered and cracked, but ultimately popped out of the car without shattering, the glass itself being more durable than the frame in which it sat. The metal groaned as rivets and bolts popped out, and the car kept moving forward despite the obstacle in front of it. The front of the car even wrapped slightly around the swashbuckling hero, as if the car wrapped itself around a pole. But even a pole or lamppost wouldn't have been able to resist several tons of bulletproof and reinforced truck flying at it with such speed. And so the unstoppable force met the immovable object.

The Magnificent stood his ground. He'd been hit, shot at, and run over enough times to know a hit like that wouldn't hurt him. Gone was the timidity he'd felt fighting his first fire. After he'd lifted up a few buildings, a little thing like a car crash wasn't going to phase him anymore.

Maxwell looked giddy, and even applauded. "Oh, perfect!" he shouted. "Right there!"

"Please," said the Magnificent, stepping forward with a single hand out as if calming a wild dog, with care but without malice. "I don't want to hurt you. I don't know how you're doing this, but you can't abuse your gifts like this."

"My name's Maxwell," says the villain, taking a step closer to the Magnificent. "I want you to know it. I'm not some one-and-done thug. We are going to have so many great fights. I can't wait to kick your $#!!+ around the block."

"That's…really not going to happen," said the Magnificent, trying to sound tough to cover what was, frankly, confusion.

"You might be tough," said Maxwell, static electricity starting to crackle between his fingertips. "But I had a thought…"

Electricity arced out of the fingers of both of his hands and into the Magnificent. The young hero screamed while his head jerking back as his muscles twitched, quivered, and pulled him in every direction. The electricity flowed out of Maxwell's scalp and up his hair as the light show in front of him reflected in the mirrored lenses of his purple shades. He grinned as arcs of electricity wrapped around and around the Magnificent. The screaming made it even better.

The Magnificent dropped and hit the ground as the surge of electricity stopped. On his hands and knees, he felt the warm trickle of blood rolling out of his ears and down his cheeks. He heard the slight drip of blood from his nose splashing on the ground in between gasps for breath. With his eyes squeezed shut he couldn't see Maxwell crouch down next to him.

"I thought, that much voltage of electricity is going to leave you sore no matter how stylishly you dress."

He waited for a response, as the Magnificent continued to heave in pain. "I'm sorry, mate," said Maxwell. "I meant to be more gentle the first time. I got carried away."

Outside the bank, Captain Bentley and his officers regrouped. The FBI charged in and officially took over the scene, but despite the fancy command station their special agents set up, most of the Bureau's firepower had just disappeared into the bank. The fact the Magnificent followed them inside and still none of them returned bode very ominously for their collective fates. Bentley would fear the worst if he didn't see the agents or the young hero soon.

Bentley regretted his wish to see the Magnificent as soon as it came true. An enormous eruption from the side of the building shook the already rattled police veteran, when a medley of bricks and granite and drywall blasted outward from the building. The enormous bank vault door flew through the wall several stories in the air. It smashed into the Magnificent like a bug on a windshield.

The vault door carried the Magnificent through the air a ways before both began to tumble. They landed in the street together. The vault door pancaked, landing flat and smashing into the pavement of the dirty Chicago street, taking a chunk of a parked Nissan Versa with it. The Magnificent on the other hand bounced after he hit the ground, tumbling and rolling a bit instead of leaving a cartoonish imprint of his body in the street.

Out of the bank came Maxwell, excited now, trotting - maybe even running - to where the Magnificent landed.

"Thought you might have super senses or something!" called out the static-charged rogue. "But I guess you couldn't see that coming, could you?"

The Magnificent struggled to his feet as Maxwell approached.

"You sure can take a pounding, kid, but you've gotta give me something back here - I feel like I'm doing all the work!"

Almost as soon as he'd finished his sentence, the red-and-blue clad teenager reared back and let out a simple right straight punch.

WHAM! The Magnificent hit Maxwell square in the nose, knocking the super villain backward on onto his ass, his purple sunglasses clattering into the street beside him.

"Ow! You cheeky little bugger!" he cried, as he called the sunglasses back into his hand with invisible electromagnetic power. Disappointingly, they had cracked. "My glasses!"

"Now stay down!" said the Magnificent firmly. "Please," he added.

Behind the Magnificent, a street light popped free from the sidewalk at Maxwell's command, taking chunks of concrete with it as it flew toward the battle. The pole tilted back as if a giant, invisible being slung the lamppost over its shoulder, ready to swing. Like a giant metal baseball bat, the lamppost swung forward at the Magnificent. The blow caught him in the back of the head, so hard and so unexpectedly the lamppost cracked in half at the point of impact.

The blow threw the Magnificent forward, who hit the pavement face-first. He rolled onto his back to get up, but the lamppost planted itself square on his chest. Maxwell grinned and made a fist, and the lamppost continued to press itself downward. The Magnificent's chest was too strong to give, and the lamppost crunched into a ball, pressing itself downward and folding up like an aluminum can of soda squeezed from both ends.

The attack left the Magnificent out of breath. It turned out even an invincible superhero needed to breath. Maxwell stood tall above the young hero, and raised his hands into the air. The crunched up metal ball which used to be a lamppost rose into the air above Maxwell's head, joining sewer caps, a postbox, the bumper of a squad car, and an increasing amount of metal junk and debris. The debris twisted, compressing on itself, as if an unseen sculptor shaped the material.

Glee filled Maxwell's eyes as he stared at the Magnificent, his arms raised high while the teenager struggled for breath. His metal masterpiece formed above his head as he called out, "Maxwell Edison! You know, kid! Like the song?"

Maxwell threw both of his hands down in front of him, calling down his creation: the metal debris formed into the shape of a giant silver hammer.

BANG! The hammer came down and struck the Magnificent. The pavement beneath him gave under the pressure, smashing the hero into the street. BANG!

"Yeah, take it!"

CLANG! Maxwell's hammer continued to pound the Magnificent. The rogue waved his hands again, swinging his giant hammer at the young hero once more.

CLANG! The hammer stopped in the Magnificent's hand. The young hero caught the hammer mid-swing. Maxwell felt surprised for a moment, but not as surprised as he felt when the Magnificent immediately followed his all-star catch with a shove to Maxwell's chest. The force sent Maxwell flying backward, tumbling through the air, and slamming backward into the door of a police squad car.

The sun hung low in the air now, the sky filled with orange and purple haze from the city's light pollution. The glare of the setting sun almost made it impossible for Maxwell to see the Magnificent flying at him, charging to press the attack.

Maxwell, dazed from the last shock and blinded by the sun in his eyes, cast a hand outward blindly. An enormous spray shot electricity in arcs in every direction, hoping to get lucky. Sure enough, the Magnificent flew right into the crackling energy, and dropped out of the air like a rock, writhing.

"Say my name," said Maxwell, walking over to the crumpled body of the Magnificent. The young hero shook his head, and with two fists extended upward he took off again. Flying straight upward into the sky.

For a second, Maxwell panicked - was the Magnificent leaving? So soon? They'd only just gotten started!

"Where are you going?!" he shouted.

Maxwell put his palms out to his sides, and lifted his arms up until they were parallel to the street. The squad car which had just broken his fall took off after the young hero, along with the remains of a silver Nissan Versa which somehow ended up with a bank vault door on it (of all things). The two cars approached the Magnificent from either side, and smashed together, sandwiching the young hero in between them.

"I've been so bored for so long!" Maxwell said as he released his grip, lowering his fists to his side. "Then, I saw you on the telly!"

The two cars, unable to rely on Maxwell's magnetic personality to hold them aloft, succumbed to gravity and fell limply to the ground. There, between them, unable to fly, the Magnificent plummeted downward.

"And I knew we were meant to be. We'll be doing this for years!" Maxwell went on as the Magnificent crashed to the ground. Hard.

"Because I'm your *perfect enemy*," Maxwell said as he grinned.

"That was so good!" yelled Maxwell, jogging over to the Magnificent. "Now, I want you to give it to me again, real hard!"

The Magnificent lay silently in the street.

"Wait, I…is that it? You're finished?"

Again, silence.

"Oh bugger me! That's all you've got? I flew all the way from London! For this?!"

Maxwell started at the Magnificent, and the only motion was a babbling brook of blood drizzling from the young hero's lips.

Maxwell stepped up and onto the Magnificent's chest. Grinding the heel of his converse into the hero's chest emblem, Maxwell asked, "How were you not ready for this?"

"You dressed up and put yourself out in front of the whole world. You didn't think someone would try and knock you down a peg? That's what *happens* when you dream big. I mean - you're wearing a #*&$!%@ cape!"

Maxwell leaned in even closer.

"You were asking for this."

Maxwell stood up, turned around, and sauntered toward the armored car, rolling out of the bank and down the street, no driver in the crushed cabin behind the demolished engine block where the truck had slammed into the Magnificent.

"Sorry I made a mess!" he called back. "Loser cleans up! Ha ha!"

Maxwell stepped up onto the trashed engine block, and hopped up onto the top of the car. As it began to rise into the air, ready to fly across the city, Maxwell Edison turned to look back at the Magnificent.

"Seriously though," he said. "Next time? You'd better *man up*."

He pointed a finger down at the broken hero and yelled, "You #*&$!%@ disappoint me!" Then, Maxwell sat down, and the armored car beneath him flew off into the sky and into the setting sun.

Chapter 5
Revelations and Realizations

2 Years After the Event. Blackstone Bravo Base. Location Unknown.

"What are you implying?" the General asked.

"I imply nothing. I'm saying it outright: you disappoint me, General."

The General stood in the Magnificent's interrogation room, trying not to wretch at the smell of burnt hair and charred flesh. The sterile scent of the bleach the janitors used to clean the tiled floor of blood, sweat, and vomit only made the odor that much more nauseating.

Presently, the Magnificent lay completely unconscious, in between some serious interrogation sessions, while Dr. Gray and his men tended to the boy's wounds. After being pushed so hard for so many days in a row, a little maintenance was necessary to keep the boy alive before the experiments could continue. His wounds needed to be closed, his body pumped with antibiotics to prevent infection, and topical anesthetic applied to any burns or surgical incisions to keep the boy from going into shock.

Cameras surrounded the apparently sleeping superhero, who rested lamely in only his boxer briefs, bound at the ankles and knees to the cold steel of an operating table. But this time, a large monitor had been rolled in to teleconference directly with the General's boss. Adrian King was the only man the

General presently answered to, and the General was the only man not outright afraid of King.

Though the General's role at Blackstone technically made him an independent consultant - an arrangement which allowed him to keep his title, uniform, and all the trappings and security clearances associated with his rank - the man on the screen signed the checks, so he called the shots. Sure, Blackstone wasn't owned directly by King - layers of subsidiaries and shell companies constructed by an army of lawyers and accountants distanced the billionaire from the paramilitary outfit's unsavory operations. But, if one looked closely, Blackstone's parent company would eventually lead back to King, who coincidentally also happened to be Blackstone's biggest single client.

On paper, Blackstone merely provided bodyguard services for King, and acted as glorified security guards at his factories, laboratories, and other facilities. In actuality, Adrian King made Blackstone to be his weapon, an unstoppable force to carry out his indomitable will.

King sat comfortably in one of his many offices, barely visible behind him on the screen but enough so as to present a stark contrast to the Blackstone laboratory. A row of rich, cherry wood shelves held King's collection of rare books, the titles of which would give some idea as to the industrialist's personally ideologies. A decanter of what was certainly expensive scotch rested on a table behind him, next to one of those large globes of the planet Earth. From the elegant comfort of his office, King peered into the Blackstone operating room with his dark, beady eyes.

"It's been close to two years now, General," King said in his quiet, raspy voice. "You haven't been able to replicate any of his powers. We don't know who he is, how he acquired his abilities, nothing."

"That's because we didn't know what he could really do," said the General, happy to finally get the drop on King with something. Nothing escaped the seemingly omniscient would-be philanthropist King, so the General felt pride in surprising him. "We've had a breakthrough."

The crow's feet adorning King's eyes separated slightly as his eyes went wide with intrigue.

"A breakthrough?" King asked in his smoky voice which sounded more like a loud whisper than someone speaking aloud. "He looks like a corpse. Excellent progress, General."

The General grew annoyed. "Adrian, you needed my military connections and experience to run Blackstone's most sensitive operations, and I haven't let you down yet, have I? Now, we've learned the *source* of his powers!"

King pursed his thin lips, the only tell on his stone-like poker face which betrayed slight irritation with the General for talking back. Still, King became intrigued by the General's claims.

"Go on."

"We thought he could fly, that he was invulnerable and strong. But we were wrong."

"Oh?"

"Doctor Gray," the General said, gesturing to his colleague. "Would you elaborate for Mr. King?"

The thin doctor had gone completely bald since his work on the Magnificent began, but this latest breakthrough tantalized the tastebuds of his curiosity, and he overflowed with energy and excitement. Days like this made Dr. Asher Gray love his job.

"You see, those were just manifestations of his ability," said Dr. Gray. "He really only has one ability. The boy controls *barometric pressure*, with his mind. The other apparent powers were the physical manifestations of a subconscious use of his real ability."

"You've lost me," said Adrian.

"See, he increases pressure around him, *subconsciously*, making him ultra dense. He can do the same thing to augment his own strength. And by *decreasing* the pressure above him while *increasing* the pressure beneath him, he can fly - just like an airplane does!"

"You see," the General interrupted, "he doesn't even realize exactly how he's doing these things. It just happens. The truth is, there are dozens more applications for his power."

"For instance," the Doctor added, excited, "if he can move himself he could use his powers to move other objects *with only his mind*! Vacuums, weather, temperature - it's *all connected* to pressure!"

King stayed silent for a second, processing this news. "You've earned a reprieve, General," said King. "But I see here your Field Commander - Alfio Bottari - has recommended we put the Magnificent down. Why?"

"Commander Bottari feels in light of the Magnificent's true ability, he may be more dangerous than we'd ever be able to control in the event of a…containment breach," said the General. "He's not wrong about it. I recommend we terminate the Magnificent and end this operation."

"Listen carefully, General," said King, leaning in. "We didn't save the world from nuclear weapons to see it fall to *living* weapons. More are coming, and replicating his powers may be our only defense.

"I will consider Alfio's recommendation, but in the meantime keep the boy alive. He can be very useful to us - he's stronger than any of us ever imagined."

The screen went black.

"Christ," said the General. "I hate the private sector."

"How can you want to give up now?" asked Dr. Gray.

"Because," said the General. "This *boy* will never learn. He has no idea what it takes to be a man. He'll sit here in his stubborn silence until he dies."

"I think you underestimate him," said Dr. Gray. "You don't know how strong you are until you're tested. Isn't that the point of all this?"

The General huffed. He looked down at the Magnificent, whose eyes remained closed. "Maybe he's better off this way," scoffed the General.

Eight Months Until the Event. The Garfield Family Home. South Suburbs, Chicago, Illinois.

The Garfield family living room had brought so much joy to its family over the years. The soft leather sofa Adam now sat upon faced the family's television, where they would gather nightly when Adam was a child to watch movies together. Adam and his father enjoyed scary movies, but the family often chose comedies so as to include Adam's mother. Many laughs had echoed off those creme-colored walls.

A beautiful, ornate rug tied the room together in the center and provided a place for the family's dogs to rest. Adam noticed how tiny his mother's Yorkshire Terrier looked lying next to the family's huge Golden Retriever. He looked away at the stone hearth of the fireplace, holding crackling flames which had brought the family warmth so many nights. A sullen mood hung over Adam, and even the persistent nudging and simple smile of the gigantic Golden Retriever, Jack, couldn't cheer him up.

Pain ached through Adam, but the pain came as much from the electrical burns as from his wounded pride. Adam hadn't been in many fights - very few people were stupid enough to fight someone with bulletproof skin. He'd become a hero to help people, to protect them, and not to fight. He did it when he needed to, but with rare exception he hadn't gone toe-to-toe with anyone who could actually put up a very long fight, let alone actually hurt him.

But this time he'd lost, badly, and now he was hurting. The memory of Maxwell's merciless assault filled Adam's thoughts so deeply he barely noticed his father walk into the living room behind him. Adam's intense gaze on the fireplace's glowing embers broke only when he felt his father's hand on his shoulder. Adam very nearly jumped, surprised as his father's touch derailed his own train of thought.

"Adam?" asked his father, in a strong, deep, reassuring voice.

"You scared me, Dad," Adam replied, sitting up a little.

Adam's father walked around the side of the couch to face him. Only concern for his son restrained Mr. Garfield's warm smile.

"How are you doing, Adam?" his father asks.

Adam looks away. "I'm fine, alright? I wish everyone would stop asking me that."

Mr. Garfield nods. "Look, your mom and I work real hard to give you space to be who you're meant to be. Even when it doesn't make sense to us, we believe in you. We trust you to do what you know is right. But it's been a few days now, and I can't just sit by and watch you beat yourself up like this. Talk to me."

Adam grimaces. "I deserve this. I blew it. I blew it. I always hoped when it counted most, I'd be good enough. And I wasn't."

"Who said it's over?" asked Mr. Garfield, sitting down on the ottoman across from Adam's seat on the couch. His horned-rimmed glasses caught glints of the flickering embers from the fire. His high forehead crinkled with concern, but his eyes themselves showed only compassion.

"It is. I can't take anymore."

Adam's father leaned forward. "Adam, it breaks my heart to see you like this. But I never could have protected you forever. Life is full of people who want to tear you down so they don't have to rise up.

"They blame you so they don't have to blame themselves. Until one day, you start to believe them. But they can't take the fire from your heart without you."

Mr. Garfield put a hand on his son's shoulder now. "Bad things are going to happen. And when they do, we change. But we decide how we change. We can be bitter. Closed off. Or we can be wiser. Stronger. And still full of love."

Adam looked up now. His lower lip was trembling. He didn't feel sad - he felt relieved. Reassured.

"You've got a big heart," his dad went on, sitting back. "And no matter what you decide - I'll always love you."

Adam leaned forward and threw his arms around his Dad.

"Thank you," Adam whispered, almost too proud to look at him. Adam felt almost embarrassed to show his father how much those words meant to him.

But his father knew.

"I love you."

Later. Downtown Chicago, Illinois.

Chicago had really grown on Maxwell. The blues clubs, the thick Midwestern women, the ceaseless aggression of Chicago's Finest - Maxwell felt if he ever couldn't live in London, he'd make Chicago his home. As it was, Maxwell didn't plan on leaving anytime soon. He'd just gotten started with the Magnificent, and while the kid didn't quite have the stamina Maxwell hoped for, he'd given the Londoner the most fun afternoon he'd had in ages.

Maxwell's little sideshows hadn't been enough to draw out the Magnificent since their first bout. The scuttlebutt said the kid turned chicken and vanished. But Maxwell knew better. His first wife had always told him what a great judge of character he was. He knew the Magnificent had a stronger backbone than that. He figured the kid needed to lick his wounds before throwing down again.

Maxwell's patience, however, was not quite equal to his faith in the Magnificent. Even though Maxwell's composure and self-restraint preceded him, he gave up waiting and decided to go bigger to get the Magnificent to come out.

And so Maxwell Edison, in a brand-new suit from Nordstrom and a slimming knee-length peacoat from Macy's strutted down the streets of the Chicago loop. The crisp wool suit was such a dark black it seemed darker even than the night sky. And though the night sky looked pretty bright under Chicago's rampant light pollution, Maxwell certainly didn't need the purple Oakleys he wore now.

The loop was especially fun late at night, because even though the crowds were much thinner the city glowed all over, reminding Maxwell how much there was to play with. Something felt epic about a nighttime confrontation anyway. Daylight was fun because Maxwell could see a little bit more of what he was doing, but nighttime made the whole affair a little more dramatic. A little more climactic. Exactly what Maxwell wanted.

Maxwell flipped over cars, smashed open windows, and put on a merry light show to put the fear of God into some of the passersby. Someone would Tweet this eventually, he thought.

Sure enough, Chicago's finest had shown up, in force too. And Maxwell dispatched them so brilliantly even he needed to take a moment to admire his own handy work. A few of the squad cards Maxwell arranged completely upside down; one he parked in between the third and fourth floors of the ~~Willis~~ Sears Tower. Several of the officers he gave a good zapping to before letting them crawl away. All while moving gracefully, and with class.

Maxwell started to get worried the Magnificent wouldn't show up, when he saw it. A loan officer, crawling across the ground. His large belly could fool you into underestimating his strength. But despite having been hit by a flying mailbox a few minutes earlier, this single officer began to stand up in Maxwell's presence.

The dark-skinned Egyptian officer raised his sidearm, barely able to lift his arm while blood oozed from a wound in his bicep. Maxwell didn't even bother to shut him down. He even admired the constable. So, Maxwell resolved to give him a memorable death.

While the officer raised his piece, Maxwell raised his hands in the air. An arc began to crackle between his fingers, before jumping between his palms. The arc started jumping back and forth until the energy seemingly formed into a ball. It glowed bright like the sun, and Maxwell grinned at the officer from behind his shades.

The conflict engrossed Maxwell so much, he didn't hear the faint pop of a sonic boom in the sky behind him. A bright blue and red blur streaked through the sky. Though it moved as fast as a plane, it pointed downward instead of up. Maxwell wouldn't have enough time later to kick himself for not noticing the Magnificent sneak up on him from behind.

The Magnificent kept flying, with great speed but seemingly unstoppable force, dive bombing straight into Maxwell. He'd caught the Londoner totally unawares, and slammed into Maxwell from behind. Maxwell flew forward, sprawling into the street. He practically bounced off the pavement, sliding and rolling across Wacker drive.

If Maxwell had paid for his six-button, double breasted overcoat he might be upset at the tears it suffered during his rough tumble. But as Maxwell got up onto his knees and tried to stand, he couldn't help but smile as the Magnificent stalked toward him in his bright red and blues. This time, though, the hero had some sort of gray box with him, hanging around his torso from a brown leather strap.

Before Maxwell could wonder what it was, the Magnificent grabbed his coat collar, and hurled him back across the street. Maxwell grew dizzy as the Magnificent shoved him back and forth like a rag doll before he finally rolled, sprawling on the sidewalk, and rising to his feet.

"You want to play rough?!" Maxwell called out "Well, I'm…"

Maxwell extended his fingers, but found to his shock… nothing.

"You see this?" the Magnificent shouted, pointing to the blue dials and knobs sticking out of the plastic box around his waist. "This device matches the frequencies of your abilities, and emits a counter charge to cancel you out! You're powerless!"

Maxwell's eyes were wide with terror at this news. This wasn't fair. This wasn't a fight. Was it a bluff? He tried again, and nothing happened. No charge. No electricity. Nothing. The crackling, energizing burst of power Maxwell took for granted…

"What. Did. You. Do?!?" Maxwell screamed. "Where are my powers?!"

"Still want to fight?" asked the Magnificent, walking forward with purpose and renewed confidence.

The Magnificent placed his right hand over his left knuckles, and a feeling found Maxwell which hadn't visited him in years: fear.

"Oh…"

CRACK! The Magnificent cracked his knuckles.

"Bullocks."

The Magnificent never did have to punch too many people, and when he did he always held back. After all, he could pound concrete into dust - the structural stability of a human skull surely couldn't hold up under his strength. But, last time, he'd gone too easy against Maxwell and this time he wasn't going to make the same mistake.

WHACK!

The Magnificent threw a right cross, striking Maxwell square across the face. A mix of teeth and blood spilled out of his mouth as Maxwell's sunglasses flew from his face, shattering on the pavement.

WHOMPF!

The Magnificent wouldn't relent, and so as Maxwell lurched backward from his first blow the Magnificent reached forward with his left hand, grabbing the expensive wool lapel of Maxwell's suit to hold him in place. No sooner did he have hold of Maxwell than the Magnificent released a right hook - right into Maxwell's gut. He gasped as the air rushed from his lungs, running away from the pressure of the Magnificent's blow.

THWACK!

The Magnificent barely let Maxwell's head come back up for air before the young hero pulled back his left fist and threw a straight punch at Maxwell's face. His head snapped backward, and the blow nearly left him unconscious. Maxwell's knees buckled, and he fell forward - into the Magnificent's arms.

The young hero gripped Maxwell by the lapels, but wasn't satisfied. As his red cape flapped behind him, the Magnificent's head darted back and forth as his eyes looked for a way to end this fight for good....then, he saw it. A Chicago Police squad car. No one was in it. Perfect.

He lifted Maxwell off the ground, and without evening pausing to take a breath the Magnificent hurled his fallen enemy through the air - and face-first into the windshield of the police car.

The Magnificent sprinted toward the fallen Maxwell so fast, he didn't notice the crowds forming around him. Commuters interrupted on their way to Union Station had taken refuge in the surrounding businesses - Starbucks, Walgreens, the Fulcrum store - it didn't matter. But now, they emerged, and looked at awe at the Magnificent.

The Magnificent's task distracted him from the growing crowd, and he barely noticed the wail of the approaching emergency services vehicles as he stabbed Maxwell in the hip with a syringe. Maxwell looked like he was in pretty bad shape, which would ordinarily have bothered the very compassionate young hero. But this time, not so much.

He picked up the drooling Maxwell as emergency responders surrounded them both. A pair of police officers ran up to the Magnificent alongside Captain Abraham Bentley. The officers quickly grabbed Maxwell by the shoulders, using plastic zip-ties to secure his hands behind his back, while Bentley spit at Maxwell's feet.

"Great work, kid," said Captain Bentley. "What is that gizmo of yours?" he asked, pointing at the gray box with blue plastic knobs.

"It's Fisher Price, I think," said the Magnificent, who couldn't help but smile. "It doesn't do anything."

"So you bluffed him?" asked another voice.

The Magnificent turned around to see a tall, lean man in body armor and tactical gloves, with tactical goggles resting on his close crew cut. The Magnificent didn't then know Commander Alfio Bottari, but Bottari knew the Magnificent. He'd dreamed of capturing this so-called "hero", flaunting his powers in front of the whole world expecting praise. But, the brass hadn't figured out how to engage or subdue the hero yet, and so the orders were to simply collect the low-hanging fruit and regroup to form a new plan.

"I didn't bluff," said the Magnificent. "I...psyched him out.

"You see, a magnet loses its charge if you bang it enough," the Magnificent went on, too proud of himself to stop. "I hit him hard and fast so he'd temporarily used his powers. I used the toy as a prop to make him believe he'd lost his powers permanently. He got so psyched out he couldn't make them work."

"I don't get it," said Bentley.

"It was psycho-somatic," said Bottari. "All in his head."

Bentley smiled at the Magnificent. "You gave him the yips."

The Magnificent nodded, glancing over at Maxwell. "Exactly."

Maxwell, drooling, his eyes rolling from side to side, coughed, "You...you cheated. You cheated me. It's not fair..."

"I gave him a mild sedative," said the Magnificent. "Keep him under and you shouldn't have any problems."

"I'll take it from here," Bottari said to Bentley, pulling out some sort of paperwork. "You know the drill with superhumans...."

The Magnificent took one last look at Maxwell, then looked around him at the crowds gathered. He prepared to fly away when he felt a hand on his shoulder.

"Excuse me," said Commander Bottari. "I'd like to have a little chat with you. I'm with -"

"Sorry," the Magnificent interrupted, as he took off into the air. "My mother warned me never to talk to strangers!" He tried not to grin too much as the crowd cheered at the sight of his flying.

Bentley continued to bark at Bottari about jurisdiction and chain of command as Commander Bottari looked up after the Magnificent. Bentley's voice might as well have been static as Bottari dreamed about the day he'd get to choke the little brat with the silly red sheet wrapped around his neck.

Chapter 6
Don't Look Back

30 Months After the Event. Blackstone Bravo Base. Location Unknown.

The General sat at the head of his conference room table for what felt like the millionth time. In actuality, these progress reports on the Magnificent hadn't been more than weekly, at least not since the first month Commander Bottari had brought the hero in.

Alfio was here now, watching the monitors display live footage of the Magnificent as he lay on his operating table. One screen showed a team of doctors treating his wounds and cuts, while another screen showed the so-called hero's heart rate and other vitals.

BEEP. BEEP.

Alfio's eyes remained fixated on the screen, the only person in the room who remained composed. His uniform, his physique, his close-cut hair - all seemingly the same as they day he brought the Magnificent in, nearly two and a half years ago.

Dr. Asher Gray looked much worse, however. His hair had almost completely fallen out, and his eyes lay sunken and dry behind his glasses.

"Why do we have to push him so hard?" he asked, too weary to continue to placate the General. "I can do noninvasive procedures. We could earn his trust. Experiments are one thing, but torture just for torture's sake?"

"Do you know the numbers, Doctor?" asked Bottari, his eyes still locked on the screens. "About people like him?"

The Doctor nodded. "They're my projections."

"Then you know, statistically, the existence of just one - just one - of those things increases the likelihood there will be more."

"Alfio is right," said the General. "You know what a dozen people like him would do to the world. A hundred?"

Dr. Gray nodded. "It would be…catastrophic."

"You should've just euthanized him years ago," Bottari told Gray.

"And just why should I listen to you?" Gray snapped back. "Your hatred for this kid clouds your judgment. Exactly what is your problem with him?"

"My problem?" Alfio, finally turning his back on the screens, looking at Dr. Gray. "My problem is this kid is more powerful than any of us and he didn't do *spit* for it. He didn't work, he didn't train, he didn't suffer. He just fell ass-backward into superpowers."

"Commander Bottari is right," said the General. "We need to take his power and put it in the hands of those who can be trusted. Those who have been tried."

"I think it's time we start talking about dissection," said Alfio.

"Oh I didn't realize you'd been to medical school?" Dr. Gray asked Alfio with sarcasm dripping from every syllable.

"Excuse me?" said Bottari, stepping away from the screens and toward the doctor to intimidate him.

"It may come to that, if he doesn't come around soon," said the General. "But if we could learn who he was? Before all this? Where he came from? We'll get his cooperation."

The General stood from his chair, and walked over the monitors. He stood face to face with the Magnificent, separated by several rooms but connected by the television monitors. As the General glared at the young hero's sunken, drooping eyes in the glowing screen, the General said, "He's all heart. And that's his weakness."

13 Minutes Until the Event. The Garfield Family Home. South Suburbs, Chicago.

The Garfield family sat glued to the news for the last few minutes. The government raised the terror alert level only a little while ago, but what shreds of information had hit the airwaves made it clear an attack was imminent.

The unknown scares us more than anything. And so the most terrifying thing about this threat was no one yet knew the type of attack…or the target.

Mr. Garfield put an arm around his wife as they sat in their love seat, their gaze locked on the television.

"This is Ken Schmidt, reporting real time updates," said the thin, bald news anchor. His small, round glass were sliding down his nose, the anchor too frantic to even notice. "The latest reports coming in from unidentified sources inside the Air Force suggest fighter jets have been scrambled and are currently en route to various major cities across the country. Our military experts here conclude the source of the attack must be some kind of intercontinental ballistic missile."

Adam sat on the couch across from his parents, his dogs at his feet. Adam's hands were clenched in front of his face in a silent prayer, but one which brought him no comfort. With so many people praying to him for salvation, the idea of praying to someone to save him felt empty and lonely.

"Other reports indicate NEST teams across the country have already been mobilized," the anchor continued, "confirming earlier rumors the nature of the attack may be nuclear."

Mr. Garfield didn't even notice his hand shaking until his wife squeezed it, calming him.

"Adam," said Mrs. Garfield, looking over at her son. "Please…not this one. Not this time."

Adam shook his head. "Mom, I…."

"Wait, wait!" interrupted the news anchor, as if he could somehow hear their conversation. "Yes, it's - an unnamed source inside the Pentagon confirmed the President and members of Congress are being evacuated to underground bunkers. It looks like the target is Washington, D.C…."

Adam stood up. Now he knew where to go.

"Adam!" snapped his mother.

Adam looked down at where she sat on the couch.

"Mom, I…I love you."

Adam walked toward the sliding glass doors which stood between his living room and the backyard.

The golden retriever ran up behind him, barking. Jack never barked before, not like this.

Adam stepped outside and for a moment thought about looking back at his parents one last time. Instead, he looked up at the sky, crouched down, and kicked off the ground. He almost heard the pavement cracking beneath his feet as he leapt upward, but almost immediately after he broke the sound barrier. All he could hear was the sonic boom he left behind him as he tore off his jacket, the "m" on his chest glistening in the sun.

As his cape unfurled and flapped behind him, Adam flew East, as fast as he could. He didn't often fly out of Chicago, but he'd gone other places in the country often enough to learn his way around. Still, at the speeds he flew the wind whipped in his eyes pretty good - it would be hard to see anything, much less a tiny missile. But he had to try.

Adam blasted forward, faster than ever before. He wasn't even sure he could go fast enough to get to D.C. 600 miles per hour…800 miles per hour, 1200 miles per hour…

Adam kept pushing himself, forward, faster.

Can't look back….don't look back…

1500 miles per hour…2300 miles per hour…

He was closing in now, he could feel it.

ZOOM! Was that an F18 that just flew by? No time to stop and check.

2700 miles per hour…4000 miles per hour…

He needed to start slowing down because there didn't seem to be a limit to how fast he could go and he might risk overshooting the city if he continued to accelerate. As he slowed, his eyes darted to and fro - but with no radar, no super senses, it might be nearly impossible to…

There! There it was! The missile! But still so far away. The city was right below them both. Adam blasted forward again, as fast as he could. If he could only reach it in time…

For a split second - just a split second - Adam thought he saw the missile break apart. Instantly, he closed his eyes and shielded them with his arm, never slowing down. The flash from the explosion would have blinded him but for this, though a lot of good it did him when he flew into the shockwave headfirst. He wouldn't have been able to stop anyway, and at well over a thousands miles an hour Adam hit the wave.

He didn't see the loud, white flash get so bright it blotted out the sun. He didn't see the huge crater instantly vaporized below, or the searing pulse of power bringing buildings to rubble. He didn't see the embracing lovers turned to bone, then ash. He didn't see the cars lifted off the ground and thrown through the air, breaking apart as they flew, melting in the air from the heat. He didn't see the pavement start to boil, the monuments fall, or the people die.

Adam flew backward, thrown almost as fast as he'd been flying. But it didn't feel like flying anymore, it felt like falling. And Adam fell for what felt like forever…then SLAM!

Adam hit the ground. Hard. But he didn't stop there - he left a skid mark. Like a glacier tearing up a continent, Adam left a long gash in the ground before the piling rubble finally slowed him to a stop. Everything went dark.

Time passes.

The purple and orange glow over the horizon could have been mistaken for a sunset, if it weren't the middle of the night. In the distance, the faint outline of a mushroom cloud still hung in the sky like a specter. The Magnificent lay still, motionless.

Over the hilltop, there came one at first. Then two. Then more.

Commander Bottari ran hills like this many times in his training, and despite the fact his rank meant he had a few years on the Blackstone operatives around him, he still overtook most of them in a sprint. Even with the heavy radiation-protective hazmat suits, Alfio's strength and singular focus carried him up the hill, passed his soldiers, and right to what he'd always been waiting for.

With a hand signal the Commander told his men to hold their positions.

"Call for evac, now," ordered Alfio. "And radio Bravo base to let them know we need EMTs standing by. We've got him."

Alfio didn't smile, but he'd be lying if he said he wasn't thrilled. He'd been waiting for this moment for a long time.

"Hello, Adam."

Chapter 7
Owner Of A Broken Heart

Three Years After the Event. Blackstone Bravo Base. Location Unknown.
"Hello, *Adam*."

At first, Adam thought he was just hearing things. It wouldn't be the first time. Over the years, he'd seen his mother, his ex-girlfriend, even mistaken some of the scientists for old teachers from his high school back home. But as he slowly realized the voice he heard came from right in front of him, Adam's eyes went wide. His heart nearly skipped a beat as he looked up to see the General.

Adam tried very hard to restrain himself, but the myriad monitors he remained hooked into gave away the slightest fluctuations in his vitals. For a long time now he'd kept the ultimate poker face, never opening his mouth except to scream. Even that he stopped doing a long time ago, suffering his torment with increasingly erie silence. But things just changed.

"That's right," said the General, stepping forward, a touchscreen Fulcrum tablet in his hand. "I figured out who you are. After three years of searching high school year books, and a little detective work…it's all right here."

The General's worn, leathery face looked even more grotesque now as it contorted into a huge grin. Adam had seen the occasional smirk here and there, but this time the General looked like he'd just arrived at Disneyland.

90

Dr. Gray, Professor Shapovalov, and Commander Bottari were all there. None of them would miss this moment.

"Adam Garfield. Born and raised, suburban Chicagoland. Mom, Dad, two dogs - wait, one dog. Your golden retriever died. Sorry."

Adam's lip began to tremble.

"Good student, nice kid. Hell, I'm surprised you weren't in the damned glee club. Oh wait, you were a little busy for extracurriculars, weren't you?"

The General stepped forward, and reached a hand behind Adam's head. He grabbed Adam's hair and yanked, hard. Adam winced as the General leaned in close.

"Now you listen to me," the General growled through his grin. "You work for me now. When I say fly, you ask how high. You're going to tell us everything about you and you are going to play *nice* from here on out."

Adam, for the first time in three years, made eye contact with another human being and glared at the General.

The General continued monologuing, not noticing at first exactly what was staring back at him.

"If you don't help me now, I'm going to send my soldiers to your home. They're going to bring me *mom* and *dad*. And you're going to watch me hurt them, just like I've hurt you."

The General paused a moment - just a moment - as he felt the rage emanating from Adam's gaze.

"So, what do you *say*?"

Adam opened his mouth, and tried to speak. At first, all that came out was guttural, cracked - like gravel was stuck in his throat.

"Ergh….Agh…..you…ugh…"

The General released Adam's hair, and continued to smirk. "I guess three whole years of not using your vocal cords would make it sting a little, huh?"

"Argh…you…I…I've had a lot of time to think," said Adam. The General almost jumped out of his dress boots with joy. Behind him, Commander Bottari clenched a fist silently at his side in triumph.

"And?" the General pressed, too eager now to stop.

"What happened…in D.C…was an inside job. Had to be. Not my fault. Yours."

The General paused now. This time, it was his heart skipping a beat. "What?"

"'Knew exactly where the missile was.' Your words. I saw the missile. Not big enough…came from within our borders. Came from here. Inside job. From a *traitor*."

The General's grin was gone. His lips pursed tight together, his teeth clenched, and he lost control. And after three years of trying to break the Magnificent, with a few words, the young hero had broken him instead.

"You piece of $#!!+!! What the hell do you know?!" the General screamed. He hurled his tablet across the room, and it shattered.

"You have no idea - *no idea* - what it takes to be a real hero! Do you know how many lives we *saved* by sacrificing

D.C.? Can you even begin to guess *why* we would do such a thing?!

"Being a real man means doing things, terrible things, *unforgivable things* for the greater good! But you don't *get it* because you're just a *dumb kid* who thinks a cape and a mask makes you a hero!"

Adam remained composed as the General screamed.

"I never wore a mask," said Adam.

"What?" the General snapped.

"I never wore a mask," Adam said, "because I have nothing to hide. No mask, no uniform, no *title* makes you who you are. My actions define me. As have yours."

SLAP!

The General struck Adam with a swift backhand.

"How *dare* you judge me?!" the General screamed. "When are you going to *grow up*?!"

The General turned to storm out of the room.

"Doctor Gray! Give him the full dose. Of *everything*."

"General, sir, we - "

The General stopped on a dime and turned. If Doctor Gray didn't know any better he might have mistaken the General for the devil himself.

"That was *not* a request!"

The Doctor hesitated again.

"I want to hear him *scream!*"

Commander Bottari stepped toward the Doctor, a hand on his sidearm in its holster. The message was clear. Dr. Gray acquiesced.

"Throw the *goddamned switch!*" yelled the General.

He reached a hand toward the console, and turned the dial.

The machine began buzzing and glowing. Thunder ripped through the room as electricity surged through wires and needles into Adam's muscles.

"ARRRRRGGGHHH!!!" he shrieked.

Adam clenched his eyes shut from the pain, and when he opened them, it was years ago.

6 Months Until the Event. Oak Wood Nature Preserve. South Suburbs, Chicago.

Adam gently closed his eyes, tilting his head back slightly to feel the breeze on his face. As he took a deep breath and opened his eyes, Adam noticed the air tasted almost sweet this far away from a city.

"What a perfect day," Erika said, sitting in front of Adam and leaning against him. "I think we really needed this."

He didn't mind the cool breeze because Erika felt warm in his arms. The two sat on their picnic blanket, looking at the sun setting behind the trees. The sky seemed to glow, the sun only barely beginning to set.

"I finally have you all to myself," she went on. "Just you and me. I love you so much."

And yet for all the tranquility of this moment, it was still there. That heat in the back of his throat. The slight queasiness in his stomach.

Erika filled him with the same anxiety he felt before facing an opponent, in those moments when he braced for an attack. And yet, the worse the anxiety got, sometimes the only thing which made it any better was being with her. And Adam felt like any day now, he would break from this tug of war in his heart.

"I love you too, Erika," he said. "I wish it could be like this all the time." These moments of peace had become too few and far between these last few months.

"It can be," she said, almost under her breath, her impatience leaking through.

"Erika," he said, knowing she would try and talk him out of being the Magnificent yet again. "I can't — "

"Shut up, Adam," she said, trying to sound playful. "Just *enjoy* this. Relax."

Adam once tried to run from a fight, when he'd squared off with Maxwell in Uptown. For his effort, Maxwell sandwiched him between two cars. Adam hadn't run from a fight since. He'd learned the hard way, as always, the longer you let a problem fester the harder it would be to solve later.

"Erika, please. We have to work this out."

It happened like it always did. One of them would try and start a conversation. The other would take something out of context. The suspicion set in quicker every time they did this dance - interpreting each other's words in the worst possible way. Assuming the most sinister motives.

Then, Erika would start going further and further back. She knew all of Adam's sins, carved them in stone, and recited them to him. And he'd sink right down to her level - he knew his own litany by heart.

And meanwhile, minutes turned to hours.

Night fell by the time Adam flew Erika home, hovering behind her backyard where the trees were high enough to cover his descent. He lowered into the alleyway behind her backyard.

"I didn't mean for this to be another fight," he said. "But I just can't do this anymore."

"Stop," she demanded. "You'll be back in a week. You can't walk away from me."

BEEP.

"I can't take this anymore!" he snapped back. Things had only been getting worse. It started with one bad day. Then it became a monthly recurrence. Monthly turned to weekly. Now the bad days severely outnumbered the good.

"I'm nervous all the time," he said, unable to stop the flood any longer. "When I'm with you, I can't stop thinking about who needs my help right then. But when I'm out there, I'm always distracted. Wondering where you are, what you'll say. Honey, it's a mistake to keep…"

"I am *not* a mistake!"

"I didn't say that!"

"I love you!"

"Don't — " But before he finished, she kissed him. He had to push her away.

BEEP.

"No," he said. "Love is *not* ownership."

"That's not fair!"

"I'm not trying to be — "

"Please," she said, crying now. "Don't give this up."

This too was part of the cycle. When Erika could, she'd push Adam to the point of tears, even hysterics. But when he

96

stood his ground, she'd shift tactics - she'd start to cry, and play off his pity. Soon he was too busy consoling her to notice all of his own pain anymore.

"You only talk like this when I'm leaving, so I'll stay," he said. "But I can't."

Erika looked away suddenly, as if Adam had slapped her. "Stop it, stop it…"

BEEP.

Erika pulled Adam close now, and he was so weak he couldn't resist her. She kissed him, and he kissed her back, like his life depended on it. They lingered awhile, longer than normal, because they both knew when this kiss was over so were they.

"Please," she begged. "Don't go."

Adam knew if he kept talking they'd just keep going around in circles. He realized this was a fight he'd never win. And he'd never say everything he needed to, because she'd never hear it. His feet began to leave the ground.

BEEP.

"Come back here!" she shouted as he rose higher.

BEEP.

"Come back," she said, softly now, too sad to scream anymore.

As Adam floated away, Erika watched him disappear into the night sky. Erika looked so beautiful, standing there. And as Adam got further away, it got harder and harder to see her…and everything got blurry….so blurry now…

BEEEEEEEEEEEEEEP……

"He's flatlining! Get him off that thing, now dammit!" screamed Doctor Gray, years later.

Three Years After the Event. Blackstone Bravo Base. Location Unknown.

Dr. Gray frantically moved around the table, checking the myriad monitors hooked up to the Magnificent. But they all said the same thing: the boy was dead, and soon he'd stay that way for good.

"You prick, I thought you knew what you were doing!" screamed one of the guards.

Dr. Gray grabbed the paddles from his AED machine as his assistant set the charge.

"He's never had this reaction before," said the Doctor. He rubbed the paddles together.

"Clear!"

ZAP!

The electricity blasted through the Magnificent's chest. The heart rate monitor continued to ring - steady, constant, and flat.

"Doctor!" shouted the guard, grabbing Gray's arm. "The General's standing order is not to resuscitate."

"I'm *not* going to just let him die!"

"I will stop you," said the soldier, drawing his sidearm.

"You neanderthal!" the doctor shouted. "I've got three years of *my life* dying on this table! Now clear!"

ZAP!

As the Doctor zapped the Magnificent again, the soldier aimed his weapon and disarmed the safety with a loud SNAP!

"Get me the epinephrine!" Doctor Gray shouted.

"Doctor Gray, that's *enough!*" the soldier snapped back.

"You listen to me!" the Doctor shouted back. "We *just* got our hands on his family. We're about to get everything we need - if the autopsy comes back empty do *you* want to be the one to tell the General?"

The assistant handed the Doctor the syringe of adrenaline he'd asked for.

The Doctor took the syringe and glared at the soldier, who hesitated only a moment, his eyes darting back and forth from the syringe to the dying super-hero.

"Do it!" he yelled.

WHUMPF! Doctor Gray brought the syringe down into the Magnificent's chest...hard. He looked up at the heart rate monitor, still ringing.

Dr. Gray's eyes were fixated on the screen, compressing the Magnificent's chest over and over. The placid expression on the young hero's face came from the first peace he'd known in years.

Then, the heart rate monitor stopped ringing.

* * * *

BEEP!

Suddenly an invisible force hurled Dr. Gray through the air. The lab assistants recoiled as the guards scrambled to draw their weapons. The doctor shrieked as gravity lost its hold on him, and he tumbled backward through the air, crashing into the unforgiving coldness of the ceramic floor. The cameras, monitors, and equipment started to burst, their screens and lenses shattering with sparks as they tumbled over. The mannequin wearing Blackstone's red-and-black "Magnificent" uniform, the lab equipment, and trays of surgical instruments flew into the air, the latter bending and contorting like an invisible car had run them down.

The Magnificent sat up now, jerking and thrashing as his leather straps snapped, useless and limp. The guards would have had their guns on him by now but the invisible force returned, picking each of them up and into the air, where they slammed together before dropping to the ground like popped balloons.

One of the lab technicians was too scared to move, but the other frantically tried to subdue the Magnificent with a shot of barbiturates, probably out of habit rather than courage. The Magnificent picked the lab technician up with one hand and lifted him high into the air and over the Magnificent's head.

Years of eating through tubes and IVs left the Magnificent with almost no body fat, and though he didn't have much muscle mass either he looked cut as his muscles tensed and contracted before slamming the lab tech down onto the operating table. The Magnificent's shoulder and bicep bulged as he pulled back his left fist, and his tricep flexed as he jabbed forward in a devastating blow which struck the lab tech square in the sternum. The tech stopped writhing.

The Magnificent tuned to the other lab technician and extended a hand. Suddenly, several feet away, the Magnificent's will traveled through the air, slamming into the other technician and throwing him backward and off his feet, where he landed hard and his head snapped back and into the ground.

Finally, the screams stopped, and everything calmed down a moment.

Adam stalked forward, wearing only the red trunks which preserved his remaining dignity for the years of his captivity. Adam used his newfound abilities to vacuum seal the doors to the room shut, and they could not have been opened any more easily than a door on an airplane mid-flight.

Adam's surprise at his newfound mobility was surpassed only by the jittery, uncontrolled energy in his body. Years of operating through the haze of tranquilizers had made him perpetually exhausted, dizzy, weak, and nauseous.

As he walked passed the two guards, trying to get up off the ground, Adam pointed his fingers at them with a flick of his wrist. Their heads slammed together with a POP like coconuts.

Adam crouched down next to the Doctor, scrambling on the floor to find his spectacles. Adam smirked.

"Hello, Dr. Gray."

"Pu-please…" the doctor stammered. "Don't - "

"Shut. Up."

The doctor's lip began to tremble. After all these years, he'd stopped thinking of Adam as a person. It made it easier to conduct his tests, to poke and prod and ponder if the Magnificent was just some lab rat, or better yet some automaton, rather than an actual teenage boy. Of course, he wasn't much of a teenager now, three years after the fateful day the Commander took him prisoner.

"We sedated you…" the doctor said, hoping as much for a reprieve as he was for answers, the truth he always sought at all costs. Maybe now at the cost of his own life.

"You were right, the sedatives kept my powers at bay," said Adam, crouched down close to the doctor, unafraid and unhurried. "When you helped me find out what I could *really* do, it took years of practice to use those powers internally. I was finally able to hold my heart in place, and kill myself. The General wouldn't need my family if I were dead."

Adam stood now, tall. "When you revived me with adrenaline, you counter-acted the sedative and my powers returned."

"But…how?" asked the doctor.

"You were right about pressure," said Adam. "I know you're a biologist, but I've always been kind of a physics nerd. Do you know how much I can do now? How powerful I really am?"

As Adam turned his back to the doctor and walked away, he raised a single hand. The mannequin, adorned with the tactical version of his old costume, began to rise off the floor.

"I mean, but how did you know we'd use the adrenaline to revive you?" asked the doctor.

"I didn't," said Adam as he raised his other hand, lifting shattered bits of mirror off of the floor. The shards quivered as they hovered in front of him, and he inspected the stubble on his face. Blackstone shaved him many times, maybe for medical reasons or maybe for hygiene, who knows. Now he didn't have a long beard, but his face was definitely obscured.

"The plan was to kill myself, but fate intervenes," said Adam. "So the plan's changed."

The doctors eyes went wide.

"What - what's the plan now?"

"I'm going to give you what you wanted. I'm going to show you what I can do."

Chapter 8
The Student And The Master

Blackstone's security coordinator didn't notice the General walk up behind him. Normally the "independent consultant" took over any room he entered, but the coordinator's eyes were glued to the monitors in front of his seat. The alarm screeched, incessant, and some of the flashing emergency lights in the hallways turned his monitors into strobe lights. He pondered the usefulness of such emergency signals, but only for a moment before returning to his duties.

"How long ago?" asked the General.

"About ten minutes now," said the coordinator, while other soldiers and security personnel frantically ran about the room.

"Where is Doctor Gray? Professor Shapovalov?"

"Doctor Gray is in there with the Magnificent," said the coordinator. "All the cameras went dead, so the Doctor is…I mean, I don't think he made it. Professor Shapovalov left the grounds just before the lockdown."

"That sonuvabitch," said the General, angry and glad to have someone to blame. "He knew about this, and left before I could lock the place down. I'll cut that coward's throat next time I see him. But at least Dr. Gray got what he deserved."

"General, this is Commander Bottari," came a voice over the intercom. "Requesting permission to implement my containment protocols."

"Do it," said the General. "Put this brat down, for good."

All around the Blackstone base, soldiers sprinted to and fro, arming themselves and suiting up their body armor. Combat boots pounded the pristine, sterile ceramic floors. Rifles clanked against kevlar as the soldiers sprinted into position.

Two sets of those boots rounded one of the hallway corners, racing to assemble at their post. But, as the lead soldier took his first step around the corner, his feet missed the ground. Suddenly, his steel-toed boots were over his head, and he flew through the air and slammed into the far wall of the hallway. The second soldier didn't have any time to react before his head snapped back and his feet flew out in front of him. He fell backward, clothes-lined by some invisible energy, and landed hard on his back, his helmet cracking against the unforgiving linoleum floor.

The Magnificent stood above the broken soldiers, like a statue. His expressionless gaze and dead eyes might've chilled the two soldiers, but they were gone now. The Magnificent floated down the hallway like a specter, his feet never touching the ground. If he was surprised by the sight of a third soldier rounding the corner, he gave no indication. Even when the soldier fired a three-round burst out of his semi-automatic rifle, the Magnificent didn't so much as flinch as the armor-piercing rounds bounced harmlessly off his new black-and-red uniform. The Magnificent simply stretched out one of his hands - the soldier flew backward, while his rifle flew forward and clattered on the ground.

As the Magnificent hovered through the halls, for a brief moment he wished he still had a cape when suddenly a door opened beside him. A single bald soldier stood, frozen in place; clearly, he hadn't expected to happen on the escaped prisoner. The Magnificent didn't even turn his head to look at him and just held up a single hand. The bald agent of Blackstone thought he heard a pop before he felt his nose start to bleed. He collapsed to the ground in a heap.

In the control room, things went from bad to worse. At various stations, analysts ordered soldiers into position, while others coordinated the distribution of ammo and weaponry. The General and his head coordinator were glued to the monitors with a few other agents.

The General looked up and around. Four analysts each watched a half dozen monitors cycling through countless cameras, positioned on every floor and at every nook and cranny of the facility.

"There he is, sir!" yelled the General's lead security coordinator. The General looked at the monitor, and his heart nearly skipped a beat when the Magnificent looked up at the camera before floating away.

"He's leaving all the cameras on, purposefully," said the General. "That little - he wants me to watch."

"He's too powerful!" shouts one of the analysts. "We're trapped in here - game over, man. GAME OVER!"

"I do not have time for your personality disorder, solider!" snapped the General. "You shut your mouth and keep it together!"

The General watched the Magnificent, floating from a camera on one monitor to another, as if he were teleporting from screen to screen.

Commander Bottari joined the General now. "Scared yet?"

"You *watch it*, Bottari!" the General barked. "It'll be fine! Alpha team —"

"Is already dead," said Bottari, like ice. "They're a diversion."

"They'll be fine!"

"We'll see. I'm taking Bravo team into position."

In the mess hall, two dozen soldiers waited for the Magnificent behind overturned tables and tipped-over vending machines. The soldiers trained all of their weapons on the double doors to the mess hall.

They could barely hear their field commander give the order to fire because the terrified soldiers pulled their triggers the second the Magnificent knocked both doors open and walked into the room.

Smoke began to fill the air as the deafening rat-tat-tat of the Blackstone semi-automatic rifles made the room shake. The soldiers pulled their triggers in successive, short, controlled bursts over and over again until one by one their barrels glowed red hot and their ammunition ran out. Hundreds of lead rounds pierced through the air, ready to shred the Magnificent's flame-retardant, segmented black armor and mirror-like 'M' chest shield. The bullets raced forward at first - then, they slowed to a crawl, and then a to a complete stop.

The Magnificent didn't smile. He didn't grin, smirk, or wink. He didn't growl or snarl, he didn't look at the bullets floating lamely in the air, nearly too many to see through. No, he just stood there, as devoid of anger as he was of every other passion. Then, the bullets began to drop. The clanging of all those bullets raining on the floor sounded like a cymbal rattling around, as the Magnificent floated backward and out of the cafeteria.

As he watched the soldiers nearly drop their guns in awe, *then* he smirked.

And the doors slammed shut.

"General!" yelled a pudgy, fair-haired soldier glued to the security monitors. "Look, quickly!"

"What is it, soldier?" demanded the General, his eyes frantically searching the glow of security monitors.

"Dear God," he whispered. "Put all the screens on the mess hall, now!"

Suddenly the monitors all shifted to show the same terrifying scene from a dozen different angles. Guns, napkins, silverware, bullet casings - this and more flew around the mess hall, caught in a vortex as the air fled the room, sucked right out the door. Blackstone soldiers dropped, hitting the floor, gasping and grasping at their throats as the vacuum sucked the air right out of their lungs.

"He's pressurized the room!" yelled the security coordinator. "He's made a vacuum! God, their lungs are going to collapse!"

Few things scared the General. This horrified him. Some of the shots showed the whole room, with a platoon of Blackstone operatives collapsing and debris flying everywhere. Others showed the guards already gone, collapsed on the floor. Still other cameras caught them trying to desperately to yell out but unable to use their vocal chords without air. They wanted to beg for their lives, to call for help, to gasp their final words - but their silent screams fell like trees in an abandoned forest.

The General's eyes locked on one of these men, his mouth wide in a silent shriek, his eyes bloodshot and bulging out of his head. The General knew the operative couldn't see him through the lens of the security camera, but for an instant it seemed as though the soldier's eyes were blaming the General.

Commander Bottari took up his position along the rail of the topmost floor. The huge, round center of the building provided him a perfect ambush point. With no right angles, there'd be no place for the Magnificent to put his back to once he entered this vestibule.

As the Commander assembled his tripod for his sniper rifle, he kept an eye over the edge. Every floor of Bravo Base - or at least, the above ground floors - were circular, surrounding this single shaft in the center which ran from the vaulted glass ceiling several stories up all the way down to the marble floor below. Along the rim of each floor, the Commander's hand-picked elite guardsmen took up positions, ready to fire.

The Commander knew his men didn't have a hope in hell of taking on the Magnificent. Bullets have been bouncing off this little freak for years. The Commander had studied how to take on the so-called super-hero for a long time, even before Blackstone got their hands on him and unlocked the secrets of his powers. Now the Commander's certainty of the Magnificent's weakness emboldened him.

If only the brass had just let the Commander put this freak down when they had him sedated, all of his men would still be alive. These operative were just trying to provide for their families. These people trained and sacrificed, sweat and bled for their skills, just trying to use their abilities to provide a life for themselves and their loved ones. And now this monster marched through them all wearing the tactical armor Blackstone made for him, with one-in-a-billion powers granted to him with the freak luck of a lottery winner, waving his hands and throwing clumsy fists with no training or discipline at all. Yet the Magnificent possessed so much power his dull, untrained attacks still bested the Blackstone commandoes.

Yet he'd been imprisoned for years without real food or sunlight. The Magnificent had become emaciated, malnourished, and tired. Not to mention the constant physical agony. Surely, even he had a breaking point.

Not only was Commander Bottari counting on this breaking point, he counted on the Magnificent not knowing where the breaking point was. The mess hall had always been a distraction for this purpose, to make the Magnificent feel as though he'd won. After all, it was a logical ambush point.

And so the Commander's protocol called for the sacrifice of two dozen agents to lull the Magnificent into a false sense of surety. He'd come up the elevator any second now, the elevator poised in the crosshairs of the Commander's enormous weapon. The Magnificent's invulnerability came from the subconscious creation of a field of barometric pressure, which is why bullets never even touched him even when they appeared to. Now, caught off guard, sluggish from years of imprisonment and high off of his victory at the mess hall, the Magnificent might not react fast enough - even subconsciously - to create the field necessary to protect himself from a .50 caliber armor-piercing sniper round straight through the eye. Even if he did react, the Magnificent was never recorded to have taken a hit of that size and caliber before. Sure he'd survived a nuclear shockwave - but the concentrated force behind such a powerful shot, like a pinpoint, at just the right vulnerable point - well, the suddenness and power of the shot might be enough to take his head clean off.

At this range, the bullet would go straight through his skull before the sound ever hit his ears. His body would hit the floor before the echo even dissipated. The extra men were just there to distract the Magnificent so the Commander was sure to get off the kill shot before the Magnificent even knew he was there.

The Commander steadied his breathing, calm and ready for battle. He was a true war machine, ready for a fight to the death with the pulsing fury of a racehorse about to leave the stables, but with the calm of a zen master. He was a bolt of lightning, not a hurricane, ready to strike with incredible precision and unmatched fury.

Suddenly, it happened - the elevator chimed "ding." In that same split second, the Commander's finger moved to the trigger, steady and ready to fire when suddenly KA-BOOM! The elevator doors exploded outward violently, and the Magnificent floated through them, calm and slow.

The other men jumped. Itchy trigger fingers and nerves the Commander hadn't expected caused his men to open fire. The bullets bounced harmlessly off the Magnificent, as always, while the Commander screamed into his radio, "You idiots! Hold your fire, dammit!"

The Magnificent began to float up the center of the room, his arms outstretched to his sides. As he passed each level, the soldiers on there would fly forward, flipping over the railing and plummeting to the ground floor below. They moved as if some great force came up from behind them and pushed them over, swiftly and all at once.

This was his chance. The Magnificent was square in the Commander's crosshairs.

BLAM!

The .50 caliber armor piercing sniper round could've ripped through a fully-armored tank. When it hit the Magnificent's eye, it exploded harmlessly like a roman candle on the fourth of July.

The Commander backed up from the edge as the Magnificent rose before him, and landed directly in front of the Commander.

With a flick of his wrist, the Magnificent sent his will out before him through pressurized air, grabbing the Commander's sniper rifle and throwing it off the ledge and into the center of the room. The Commander glared at the Magnificent and tried not to flinch as he heard the sniper rifle clatter and snap against the rigid marble ground many floors below.

"Hello, Commander," said the Magnificent. "I'm ready for that little chat now."

"You freak!" Bottari yelled. "You have *no idea* what you've been handed! You're gunpowder with no barrel! I've always known you were dangerous to everyone around you. Life just *gave you* these powers, and for what? Now I'm supposed to be afraid of you?!"

In one motion of blazing speed, with the practiced accuracy of a man who'd done this thousands of times - sometimes when his life depended on it, as now - the Commander drew his sidearm and flicked the safety, taking aim and pulling the trigger, all in a single fluid motion. The range was nearly point blank, and round after round hit the Magnificent square in the face. Three shots fired off in only a second.

The Magnificent stared at the Commander. If his cold dead eyes felt anything other than utter indifference, they didn't show it. A furious rage welled up in the Commander. How dare this child look at him like that? Like he didn't matter? Like he was this insignificant thing to be ignored. How dare he?

The Commander stepped forward, pulling back his right arm, and threw a right straight punch which landed square on the Magnificent's jaw. The punch would have disfigured most people; instead, the Commander felt the bones in his hands snap and pop as if he'd punched a steal beam head on.

The Magnificent didn't flinch, but this time, his eyes showed more than disdain. This time, his eyes narrowed into an angry glare. The Commander thought for a moment the Magnificent looked....offended. Then his vision started to blur from the pain in his hand.

The General stood amongst the terrified children he'd once called soldiers as they all watched in collective horror at the carnage all around them. On every camera, some soldier fell to the ground, writhing in agony. The lucky ones got thrown into a wall by the massive wave of pressure the Magnificent threw from his hands. The unlucky ones got the air sucked out of their lungs. But the worst were those who just dropped as the Magnificent gestured at them. The General figured the Magnificent somehow gave these soldiers some kind of aneurysm but he couldn't be sure.

The security analysts locked the control room down. Because the whole base's nervous system networked to the brain in this room, the lockdown meant the room was virtually impregnable. Giant steel doors with pressurized locks protected the security analysts from the outside world. The General always used to say a tank would have trouble knocking down the door to this room. Which is why he was so surprised to see the door fly off of its hinges, knocked free by the flailing body of Commander Alfio Bottari.

As the giant steel door smashed to the ground like a car driving into the side of a building, the General saw the Magnificent in the hallway. He just recovered his balance from the devastating haymaker which just sent Commander Bottari straight through the titanium-reinforced door to the control room. And now the Magnificent walked forward and into the room.

The General drew his sidearm while the security personnel fled for the door, hugging the sides of the walls to stay as far away from the Magnificent as possible. He didn't notice them at all, his icy blue eyes locked on the General.

"We're all gonna die!" the General thought he heard someone scream. He almost didn't notice. His eyes locked on the Magnificent.

For a second, the General though he'd caught a break. His lead security consultant headed for the door with the rest of the cowards, but now he'd doubled back to catch the Magnificent by surprise from behind. The General tried to keep a poker face so as not to give it away. But his ruse proved futile - without even turning his head, the Magnificent made the slightest gesture with his right hand.

Blackstone's head of security collapsed to the ground behind the Magnificent, shrieking as his knees pounded into the floor. Blood spurted from his nose while he squeezed his eyes shut. It felt like his skull was about to explode, and he squeezed the sides of his own head to keep it from bursting. Whatever the veteran Blackstone commando once commanded, now it was all he could do to remain in command of his own bowel movements.

The General saw a great deal of violence over the course of his illustrious career. Scores of boys became men under his command, only to be struck down in their prime with a violence which defied description. No fiction had ever captured the horrors he'd seen. And yet, the General made peace with it a long time ago. People died. Soldiers get shot. The world continues to turn. It made sense to him.

But the Magnificent left the General scared, unsettled, and disturbed because nothing around him right now made any sense. The Magnificent's powers didn't make sense. A teenager slaughtering the largest private army in the world didn't make sense. And the General's heroic life and career getting cut short by this little punk didn't make sense.

Despite years of commanding his emotions, the General lost his temper twice in one day thanks to the Magnificent. It was with this rage he brought his service-issue sidearm to bear on the boy. He took aim, removed the safety and with the same motion he pulled the trigger. At least, he'd tried to - as he squeezed, the gun decided to fly out of his hand and across the room toward the Magnificent. The gun belonged to the boy now, but he wasted no time in catching it and squeezing it into a useless pile of metal.

The Magnificent reached out a hand, and the General flew backward and up against the wall. The General felt the pressure build around his throat, gripping tighter and tighter. It was as if the Magnificent actually grabbed him by the neck and lifted him up. The General gasped for breath under the force of the Magnificent's awesome might.

"Con - *cough* - congratulations, kid," the General sputtered out. "I...I knew you had it in you. *Ack*. I knew I could make a man out of you."

"Is that what I am now?" the Magnificent asked quietly, quizzically, as if talking about someone else.

"Oh, yes," said the General, nodding as much as he could with the pressure bearing down on his neck. "You've finally learned you don't get to be a hero in this world - you have to be whatever it takes to survive."

"You don't want me to be a man, you want me to be a monster. Like you."

"I'm the monster? You hypocrite. You're a killer, just like me. Well, not quite on par with me - *cough* - yet. But you killed a lot of people today, son. I'm impressed."

"I didn't kill anyone," the Magnificent said with a voice as cold as his gaze. "I knocked them around a bit...but they're still alive."

"Ha! What about the little vortex you made in the mess hall?"

"I sucked the air out of the room," said the Magnificent, gesturing to the monitors. "But only until they went down. They're out cold, but they're still breathing."

The General turned his gaze to the monitors. There, the cameras cycled through shot after shot of Blackstone soldiers stirring. They were haggard, some bloody, others dizzy...but they all stumbled up, however slowly.

"But...how did - ACK!" The General's words were caught in his throat, literally.

"Quiet, before I decide to find out if I can give you *the bends*," said the Magnificent. He walked up to the General, still firmly held in place up against the wall.

"You wanted to know my secret? You wanted to know where my powers comes from?" asked the Magnificent. "No matter what happens to me. No matter what you do to me. *I* decide who I am. I *decide* to be magnificent."

Without even looking, he gestured to the far wall. There, his powers activated a manual emergency alarm.

"And I will never become you."

A sound like the horn of an approaching barge ripped through the air, a continuous banshee wailing through the halls.

"You have 10 minutes to evacuate this base," said the Magnificent as the emergency alarm deafened the General. "Then I'm going to tear this place to the ground."

Adam stepped out of the control room, and couldn't hold himself up anymore. He stumbled, leaning into the hallway wall for support. He couldn't hold back the queasiness in his stomach anymore and he lurched forward, heaving from the bottom of his gut. He hadn't eaten solid food in a long time, so most of the what came out was sour bile. The runny yellow goo splattered on the ground in front of him, splattering onto his shiny combat boots. The colors of this costume might be a bit dark, but he had to admit, it was a comfortable fit. If he wasn't already invulnerable to harm, the armor might also have provided pretty decent protection. He wondered if one day he'd find out if the suit would insulate him from electrical attack - but decided he'd rather never risk it.

In any case, Adam stood up straight now, wiping his mouth with on his gloved hands. He moved forward, exhausted. He knew he needed to summon the will for just one more feat.

As the soldiers, scientists, and support personnel fled, the Magnificent broke through one of the glass walls on the ground floor of Bravo Base and took off into the sky. As the wind rushed into his face, memories rushed back into his mind. He'd known only pain for so long he'd forgotten what it felt like to have the freedom of flight.

Once he felt the rush of air on his face, he could feel his strength return. The exhilaration, the pure joy he felt when gravity no longer held him, made him feel confident again. And he knew he had the energy he would need. He was back.

The cool night air helped calm his stomach, too, as Adam turned about, hovering in the air, watching the Blackstone commandoes scurry about like ants. Adam stretched out his arms, glared at the base...and it started to shake.

To be honest, at first Adam wasn't sure he could do it. Using his powers like this came more naturally than he'd ever imagined, but he didn't know if he'd find an upper limit. But it didn't stop him from trying. The ground began to shudder, shockwave after shockwave rolling through the earth. Bravo Base began to rattle too, the glass walls and panels clanging in their frames.

It wasn't enough. Adam concentrated harder. The base shook more and more. The lights started to blow out. A huge crack in the earth circled the base. The ground inside the circle shook more and more and began to fall inward.

Fury filled Adam's eyes, as 3 years of helplessness all exploded out in one massive burst. He would not be helpless anymore. He would not be a prisoner anymore. He felt the warm, salty taste of blood on his lips, flowing freely from his nostril. But he wouldn't stop. Even the tinging, swelling ache in his temple wouldn't stop him.

The ground began to cave in. Bravo Base no longer stood on solid ground, but a foundation of sand and gravel. The building imploded, the roof collapsing inward as the glass walls shattered and exploded out. Smoke began to pour from the building as dust and debris shot up out of the ground and into the night sky. The entire thing folded in completely now, and a huge plume of smoke rose into the night sky.

Adam hovered there, panting. He didn't even realize he'd been holding his breath the whole time. Next time, he'd remember to breathe. As the dust settled, Adam could see where Bravo Base once stood now only an enormous crater remained. Adam hovered a moment longer, and he wasn't sure why. He didn't feel nostalgia - no, but maybe something like it. It felt more like Adam didn't know where to go next. The feeling so terrified him that for a moment he contemplated just remaining to float until he worked it out. As his mind cleared, Adam realized there was only once place to go. He just feared what he might find there.

Adam took off into the night sky, his black armor making him nearly invisible against the onyx heavens. Even the bright red "m" wrapped around his chest disappeared as he rose higher and higher.

He willed himself forward, upward, higher. He wanted to get his bearings - he didn't know for sure where Bravo Base had been located. But, the higher he flew, the less he flew for navigation and the more he flew for the fun of it. The cold night air wrapped around him, and he started to feel like his old self again.

He'd flown high - very high - higher than he'd thought he could safely. He realized he'd formed a pocket of air all around him, surrounding him and enveloping him. The air let him breathe despite the fact he'd flown higher than most airplanes dare to go, and the same air even kept him comfortably warm. Adam couldn't be sure which was more surprising: that he possessed the power to do such a thing, or that it happened subconsciously, guided by his imagination alone.

Adam looked around and could see the dark outlines of the Earth's continents against the even darker oceans lapping alongside the coasts. A billion fireflies of lights danced around the planet, as the occasional wisp of cloud rolled underneath.

Adam took a deep breath, picked a general direction toward home, and took off. A sonic boom ripped behind him, far in the distance, as he plummeted to the Earth below.

He raced through clouds, flying on his stomach with his hands stretched out before him, passed airplanes, passed the giant skyscrapers of Chicago. The air was clear and empty above his suburban home as he slowed to just a few hundred miles an hour, then a few dozen before coming to a near complete stop. He pivoted to turn upright, and floated downward feet first.

Adam floated into his front yard. His parents must have been asleep - they'd turned out all the lights off in his house. Silence echoed through the street. He walked up to the front door, and raised a hand to knock.

At that moment, fear found Adam again. What if his parents didn't live here anymore? What if the General had gotten to them? What would he say to them? Were they mad at him for leaving? Would they be happy to see him? How would it make them feel to hear about everything he'd been through? Should he even tell them? How would he explain his absence otherwise?

Adam stopped. His hand hovered there in front of his front door, a simple knock all that stood between him and home. It was right there in front of him…he just wasn't sure he belonged there anymore.

END

"But Jesus called the children to him and said, 'Let the little children come to me, and do not hinder them, for the kingdom of God belongs to such as these. I tell you the truth, anyone who will not receive the kingdom of God like a child will never enter it.'" –Jesus, Luke 18:16-17

About the Author

Carmelo G. Chimera
After Carmelo crash-landed on Earth, he grew up in the suburbs of Chicago. He co-founded Chimera's Comics before graduating from the University of Chicago Law School. Over the last two years, he's raised over $90K on Kickstarter, including funding his first graphic novel, *Magnificent*, on which this book is based.

When he's not practicing law, running his business, or writing, Carmelo likes to make custom action figures and travel the world. It's not clear if he ever sleeps. *Artwork by Gene Ha.*

Connect With Carmelo At:

www.carmelochimera.com
www.chimerascomics.com
www.chimeralaw.com
www.facebook.com/chimerascomicspress
www.amazon.com/author/carmelochimera
www.kickstarter.com/profile/chimerascomics
www.twitter.com/chimerascomics